THE SPRITE SISTERS

THE SECRET OF THE TOWERS

SHERIDAN WINN

The Sprite Sisters series

The Circle of Power
The Magic Unfolds
The Secret of the Towers
The Ghost of the Tower (Summer 2009)

First published in Great Britain in 2009
by Piccadilly Press Ltd,
5 Castle Road, London NW1 8PR
www.piccadillypress.co.uk

This book is a work of fiction. Any resemblance to
actual people living or dead is entirely coincidental.

A catalogue record for this book is available
from the British Library.

ISBN: 978 1 84812 010 5 (paperback)

Printed and bound in Great Britain by Bookmarque Ltd
Cover design by Simon Davis
Cover illustration by Anna Gould
Sprite Towers map by Chris Winn

Mixed Sources
Product group from well-managed
forests and other controlled sources
www.fsc.org Cert no. TT-COC-002227
© 1996 Forest Stewardship Council
FSC

For Char, Deb and Jill
who remember the campfires
and the old white caravan in the woods

FIELD

STABLES

SECRET GARDEN

FROG POND

SUMMER HOUSE

DOOR POND

WILD WOOD

TENNIS COURT

CONKER TREE

BIG FIELD

GATE

GATE

N

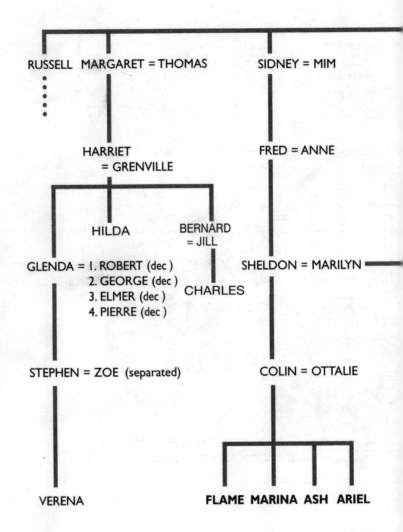

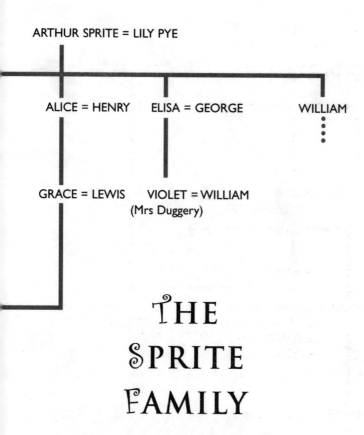

ARTHUR SPRITE = LILY PYE

ALICE = HENRY   ELISA = GEORGE   WILLIAM

GRACE = LEWIS   VIOLET = WILLIAM
                 (Mrs Duggery)

THE
SPRITE
FAMILY

This is just a small part of the
complete family tree.

THE CIRCLE
OF POWER

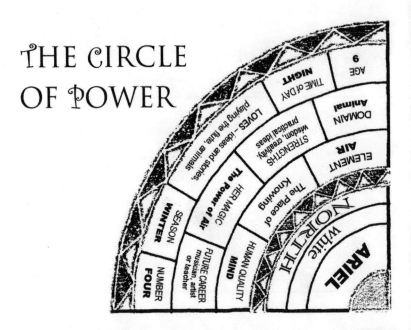

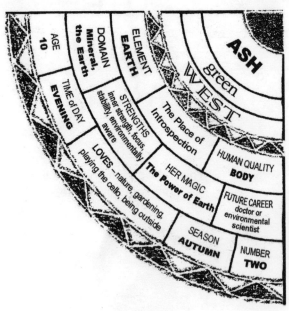

(upper wheel — ARIEL)

ARIEL

White · **NORTH**

ELEMENT AIR

DOMAIN Animal

TIME OF DAY NIGHT

AGE 6

LOVES – ideas and stories, playing the flute, animals

STRENGTHS wisdom, creativity, practical ideas

The Place of Knowing

HER MAGIC The Power of Air

HUMAN QUALITY MIND

FUTURE CAREER musician, artist or teacher

SEASON WINTER

NUMBER FOUR

(lower wheel — ASH)

ASH

green · **WEST**

ELEMENT EARTH

DOMAIN Mineral, the Earth.

AGE 10

TIME OF DAY EVENING

STRENGTHS inner strength, focus, stability, environmentally aware

The Place of Introspection

LOVES – nature, gardening, playing the cello, being outside

HER MAGIC The Power of Earth

HUMAN QUALITY BODY

FUTURE CAREER doctor or environmental scientist

SEASON AUTUMN

NUMBER TWO

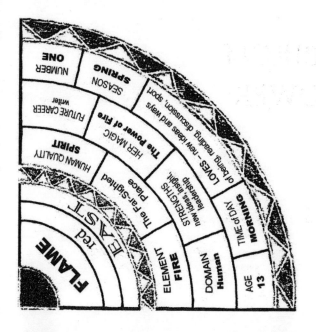

FLAME

red **EAST**

HUMAN QUALITY **SPIRIT**

The Far-Sighted Place

HER MAGIC **The Power of Fire**

FUTURE CAREER writer

SEASON **SPRING**

NUMBER **ONE**

STRENGTHS new ideas, insight, leadership

LOVES – new ideas and ways of being, reading, discussion, sport

TIME of DAY **MORNING**

ELEMENT **FIRE**

DOMAIN **Human**

AGE **13**

MARINA

yellow **SOUTH**

ELEMENT **WATER**

The Place of Feelings

HUMAN QUALITY **EMOTIONS**

FUTURE CAREER actress or singer

NUMBER **THREE**

STRENGTHS playfulness, trust, empathy

HER MAGIC **The Power of Water**

SEASON **SUMMER**

DOMAIN **Plants and trees**

LOVES – singing, dancing and acting, talking to friends, sport

AGE **12**

TIME of DAY **AFTERNOON**

CHAPTER ONE

THE

PORTRAITS

'I HAVE some interesting news,' said Dad, as he cracked open his boiled eggs at breakfast on Sunday morning in early August.

The Sprite Sisters looked up. 'What, Dad?' they asked, through mouthfuls of toast and egg.

'Sprite Towers is going to have an important visitor.'

'Who, Dad, who?' shouted the Sprite Sisters.

'His name is Charles Smythson, and he's going to make an inventory of the family portraits here at Sprite Towers,' said Dad. 'He's an art historian – and he will be staying nearby at The Oaks.'

'What – Glenda's house?' asked Flame. At the thought of Glenda Glass, the eldest Sprite Sister glowered at her boiled egg, then smacked the shell hard with her teaspoon.

Marina, Ash and Ariel giggled. Grandma caught Flame's eye and raised an eyebrow.

Dad corrected his eldest daughter. 'Glenda lives there, yes, but The Oaks belongs to her son, Stephen Glass,' he said. 'Charles Smythson is Stephen's cousin – he's a Sprite, too. He's just completed an inventory of Stephen's paintings, including the Sprite portraits from his side of the family. Stephen is keen to get all the Sprite portraits documented and he suggested that I ask Charles to do the same for our paintings. Stephen's offered to fund half the research, which is very generous of him – and he speaks highly of Charles. Anyway, your mother and I thought this was a good idea so we've commissioned him. It's a wonderful chance to know more about the paintings we have here at Sprite Towers.'

'But this chap is still staying with Glenda,' insisted Flame, staring at her boiled egg. 'She lives there, too.'

'Glenda is away for the summer,' said Dad, scooping out a spoonful of egg. 'Why are you so worried about *her*?'

The Sprite Sisters looked at one another – then glanced at Grandma. They each knew they couldn't tell Dad about the real nature of Glenda Glass: their enemy, the evil woman who tried to destroy Sprite Towers only a few weeks before. No, that would have to remain a secret between the five of them.

Thankfully, Dad was too engrossed in his breakfast and Mum in hers to notice their anxious glances.

'So when's he coming, this Charles person?' asked Marina.

'Tuesday afternoon, I think,' said Dad, munching a piece of toast.

As Dad said this, Ash heard her magic stone give a short

squeak – *Beeeep!* it went – and felt it vibrate in her pocket. What's that about, she wondered, putting her hand in her pocket and feeling the smooth, round shape of the stone. As the sister with the magic power of Earth, she was charged with looking after the stone. It went everywhere with her – and usually it was silent.

I wonder if it's telling me something, thought Ash.

She looked around the table. Had anybody else heard the magic stone squeak, she wondered. It sounded quite loud to her – but it seemed not, as everyone carried on talking.

Her thoughts were interrupted by Dad making another announcement. 'And your mother and I have a nice surprise for you!'

He smiled at Mum, who looked around the table at her daughters.

'What? What is it?' they shouted.

'Something that will arrive this morning,' said Mum. 'Something you will really like. You'll see!'

'Tell us, tell us!' clamoured the Sprite Sisters.

Mum and Dad grinned at one another, but neither would be drawn.

'What is it, Grandma?' they asked – but she would not say, either.

'You'll just have to wait,' she said with a smile.

Then Ariel burst out in a loud voice. 'Sidney says he'd like the portrait of Mim to be moved so that it's beside him. He says he misses her. Who is Mim?'

Dad spluttered and looked at his youngest daughter – and then at Mum.

Mum put down her cup and stared at Ariel. '*What* did you say?' she asked.

'Who is Mim?' repeated Ariel.

'No, the bit about Sidney talking to you,' said Mum.

'You know Ariel always talks to Sidney's portrait, Mum,' laughed Marina, pushing back her dark curly hair.

Mum shook her head and smiled. 'Yes, but what confounds me is how Ariel would have known the name Mim, unless he had answered her!'

Mum and Dad had often seen Ariel standing in front of Sidney Sprite's portrait, which hung in the hallway beside the wide mahogany staircase. The famous toffee manufacturer built Sprite Towers in 1910 and for years it had been family tradition that each night, as they passed up the stairs, everyone said goodnight to Sidney.

Mum and Dad had heard Ariel talking to her great-great grandfather's portrait, but they were unaware that Sidney actually replied.

'What a funny little thing you are, Ariel!' said Dad.

Grandma wiped her mouth with her napkin, but really it was to hide her smile. Flame, Marina and Ash giggled. They all knew about Ariel and Sidney Sprite's conversations.

Ariel crossed her arms over her chest and pushed up her chin. Her ski-jump nose stuck in the air, as she said again, '*Who* is Mim?'

'Mim was Sidney's wife,' said Grandma, buttering a piece of toast. 'She was your great-great grandmother – and a lovely lady she was, too. They were both lovely people, Sidney and Mim.'

'So, what does Sidney want?' Dad laughed. 'It's ridiculous! He's been dead for fifty-five years!'

'Sidney wants Mim's portrait to be put beside his on the wall,' said Ariel. 'He says it's important.' It was all perfectly clear to her.

Dad scratched his head and looked at Ariel. Where does she get these ideas from, he wondered.

'Where is Mim's portrait – which one is she?' asked Ash. There were many Sprite family portraits at Sprite Towers, some dating back hundreds of years. The Sprites were a big family and their history was here, on the walls of Sprite Towers. Few of the portraits were labelled, however, and the Sprite Sisters had little idea who was who – except Sidney, of course.

'Mim's portrait is in the drawing room, on the south wall,' said Mum.

'Let's go and have a look,' said Dad.

The family left the table and trooped through to the drawing room. They all loved this room – the most elegant in the house – with its high ceiling, and pale duck-egg blue walls hung with paintings. At one end was the carved stone fireplace; opposite stood the huge bookcase stuffed full of books. In the middle of the room, two huge cream sofas faced each other and on the polished oak floor lay richly coloured Persian rugs.

There was Mim Sprite, high up on the wall. The portrait showed her to be a pretty woman with a round smiley face, lively eyes and curly dark hair piled up on her head.

The Sprite family gazed up at the portrait.

'She looks very happy,' said Flame.

'She was,' agreed Grandma. 'Sidney and Mim were a happy couple. They built Sprite Towers and had five healthy children.'

'Mim has a kind face,' said Marina, staring wistfully at her great-great grandmother. 'I think she and Sidney should be together.'

'They must be!' said Ariel. 'Sidney says so.'

'Well, we can't move Sidney from his place at the bottom of the stairs,' said Dad, rubbing his chin.

'No!' said Flame. 'Sidney must stay there. He is the guardian of the house.'

'I suppose we could move Mim to the hall and put another painting up here, instead,' said Dad.

They all walked through to the hall and stood at the bottom of the wide mahogany staircase that stood at the heart of the house. There beside it, hanging on the wall, was the splendid head and shoulder portrait of Sidney Sprite, surrounded by an ornate, carved gilt frame. Sidney looked a whiskery, jolly sort of chap who'd tell good stories.

Mum stared at the wall. 'There's room here, Colin,' she said, pointing. 'We could keep Sidney beside the stairs and put Mim on the left, beside the door.'

'Yep,' agreed Dad, scratching his chin thoughtfully.

'But what shall we put on the drawing room wall to fill the gap?' asked Mum.

'How about that big landscape painting I did in France last year?' suggested Dad.

'Yes, that would go there,' agreed Mum.

'Right, well let's get started then,' said Dad, walking off to fetch his toolbox and a stepladder.

Two minutes later, he placed the stepladder in front of Mim's portrait and climbed the steps. Grandma held it steady, as Dad grasped the sides of the frame and lifted the huge painting off the drawing room wall. Below him, Mum and Flame grabbed the bottom corners of the portrait – and braced themselves as they took its weight.

'You two all right down there?' asked Dad.

'Yes,' replied Mum, sinking slightly.

'Blimey, it's heavy!' said Dad. With his hands clasped tightly around the frame, he slowly descended the steps. Together, they placed the portrait on the floor. It stood a metre and a half high.

'Look – there's something with writing on it down there,' said Ash, peering at the back of the portrait. She had a good eye for detail.

'It looks like a label,' said Flame. She bent down to peer at it, her thick copper-coloured hair falling over her face.

Just then, there was a sound of hooting outside on the drive. Bert barked loudly and ran to the front door.

The Sprite family had been so engrossed that nobody had heard the Land Rover arrive, towing a white caravan behind it. The Sprite Sisters rushed to the window and looked out.

'Ah – your surprise has arrived!' said Mum, smiling.

'What's that?' they asked.

'We've bought you an old caravan, to camp out in the summer,' said Mum.

Dad flung open the front door wide and stepped out.

'Amazing!' shouted Marina.

'Fab-fantastic!' shouted Ariel and dashed outside.

Everyone followed – all except Ash. She felt her stone vibrate again in her pocket and heard it squeak. She wanted to dash outside with her sisters, but something compelled her to attend to the stone. What is it telling me, she wondered.

She moved away from the front door, back towards the portrait of Mim, resting against the wall. The closer she got to it, the more she felt her stone vibrate. The squeaking got louder, too – as if the stone was excited.

Ash stood in front of the painting and pulled it forward, taking its weight against her body. She looked down at the back of the portrait. There, at the bottom, was the label. Below that, stuck in between the stretcher – the wooden frame that held the canvas – and the canvas itself, was something else. Ash noticed a tiny corner of paper protruding.

Outside, the Sprite family greeted Harry, who was towing the caravan behind his Land Rover. A big man with an open face, he was a friend of the family and the local farmer. It was his flock of sheep which were now grazing in the Sprites' 'Big Field' that ran the length of the driveway.

There was huge excitement and a lot of noise as the Sprites wandered around the caravan. Mum and Grandma talked to Harry, while Dad and the girls peered in through the windows.

Meanwhile, in the hallway of Sprite Towers, Ash bent down on all fours and peered behind the portrait of Mim. She knew precisely what she was after. With her left hand on the frame to keep the painting steady, she reached out with her right hand to the small piece of paper stuck behind the stretcher at the bottom. Carefully, she tugged the paper upwards. Bit by bit, it moved. All the time, the magic stone squeaked away.

'Okay, okay,' she muttered to it.

And, suddenly, there it was in her hand. An envelope. A small, stiff, white envelope made from expensive paper. It looks as if it has been there for a long while, she thought, noticing that the edges were yellow with age.

She stared at the address. It was written in ink in an old-fashioned, copper-plate hand and read, *The Sprite Sisters, Sprite Towers*. How weird that it's addressed to us, she thought.

Dad's voice interrupted her thoughts. 'Come on outside, Ash!' he shouted. 'Where are you?'

Ash stood up quickly and stuffed the envelope into the back pocket of her jeans. She would read it later. She made sure the portrait was steady against the wall, then turned and ran outside.

'Cool, isn't it!' laughed Marina, as she saw Ash's face light up with surprise.

'Wow!' said Ash, her soft brown eyes shining with delight.

Their father was standing, his arms crossed, smiling at the caravan.

'Where did you get it, Dad?' asked Ash, coming up beside him.

'I saw it advertised for sale locally,' he replied, putting his arm across her shoulders. 'Harry very kindly offered to tow it here for us.'

'Are we going to travel about in it?' asked Ash.

'No, it's too old for that,' said Dad. 'But you could camp in it here at Sprite Towers.'

'Fantastic!' said Ash.

'Where will it go?' shouted Ariel, still jumping up and down with excitement.

'The Wild Woods!' shouted Flame. 'Let's put it as far away from the house as possible!'

'Yes!' smiled Marina, nodding in agreement.

Dad, Mum and Grandma walked across the lawn to the Wild Woods, as Harry towed the old white caravan a little way up the drive. Ahead of him ran the Sprite Sisters. They stopped at the five-bar gate into the Big Field. Marina lifted up the heavy iron latch and pushed open the huge gate. Flame, Ash and Ariel shooed back the sheep and waved Harry through, as Marina closed the gate after him.

With the caravan swaying and creaking behind him, Harry drove slowly across the Big Field towards the Wild Woods. The sheep baaed and skittered in all directions, as the Sprite Sisters raced across the field to the gate at the far side. This time Ash opened the gate, while Marina, Flame and Ariel shooed away the sheep. Carefully, Harry negotiated his way through the open gateway and stopped a little way beyond it. Ash clanged shut the gate and ran to catch up with her sisters.

'Where do you want it?' called Harry, leaning his head out of the window. He waited as Colin Sprite and his daughters negotiated on the exact position of the caravan, with much deliberating and pointing of fingers. Within a minute, it was agreed.

'Just over there, please Harry,' said Flame, pointing to the track that led into the Wild Woods.

Dad nodded at Harry. 'That'll do fine, thank you,' he said.

'Okey doke,' agreed the cheery farmer and pulled away gently. A few metres later, the old white caravan arrived at its new home, nestled beside the tall pine trees. Harry unhitched the tow bar. As soon as the caravan was stabilised, the Sprite Sisters opened the door and raced in.

They jumped on the beds and squabbled about who should have which. They pulled open the cupboards, admired the little stove and ogled at the tiny loo. They didn't care that the caravan was old and scruffy.

'There won't be any plumbing down here, girls,' said Dad, poking his head in through the door. 'You'll have to use the loos in the house.'

'What about water in the taps?' asked Ash.

'Nope,' replied Dad. 'You'll have to bring down supplies.'

'What about electricity and lights?' asked Marina.

'We might be able to run a cable from the stable block,' he said, looking round.

'We don't need electricity!' said Flame. 'Much more exciting to have torches!'

'We could cook outside on a campfire,' agreed Marina.

'Good idea,' said Dad.

'And you and Mum and Grandma are not to come here unless we invite you!' said Ariel.

'Charming!' retorted Dad. 'Well, maybe we won't let you

back in Sprite Towers if it rains, eh!'

'Colin, let's go back to the house and get some coffee for Harry,' called Mum.

'Okay, love,' he called back.

Mum started to walk away, then turned and came back. 'Girls!' she called. The Sprite Sisters came towards her.

'Listen, I know that you will want to put all your things in the caravan, immediately,' she said. 'But first we must give it a good clean and air the mattresses, as they're damp.'

The Sprite Sisters groaned. 'Oh Muu-uum!' they said, with long faces.

'I'm serious!' said Mum, firmly. 'We'll get it all cleaned up today – then *tomorrow* you can bring your things down.'

'So how do we clean it?' asked Flame, eager to start.

'Grandma and I will show you after lunch,' said Mum. And she walked off, back to the house, across the lawn.

The Sprite Sisters stood there, staring at the caravan.

'Well, we could start by fencing off the camp,' said Flame.

'There are some metal posts we can string rope through in the stables,' said Ash. 'Dad kept them "for something useful".'

'Dad keeps everything!' Marina grinned. 'He's such a hoarder!'

'Well, it's very handy when you want something,' retorted Ash. She always stuck up for her father.

While the grown-ups sat on the terrace in the August sunshine, Flame, Ash and Ariel marked out the boundary of their camp. Marina painted a large sign saying, *No Grown-Ups Without Permission*, and nailed it to a post.

'That should keep them out,' she said.

'Yeah, right!' laughed Flame. 'You really think that'll keep Mum out?'

'Well, we can try!' Marina replied.

After Sunday lunch, Mum and Grandma and the Sprite Sisters set to cleaning the caravan. They carried out the mattresses and leaned them up against some trees, to air in the sunshine. They took down the curtains for washing. They scrubbed and swept, polished and rinsed the old white caravan until it looked as good as new – well, almost.

'Right,' said Mum, when it was all finished. 'Leave the mattresses out while the sun is shining, but make sure you bring them in before it gets damp. You can bring down your supplies and bedding tomorrow.'

Meanwhile, in the vegetable garden, Dad was busy gathering salad leaves, runner beans and courgettes. When the cleaning was finished, Ash ran to help him and the two of them spent a happy hour together. They spent some time attending to their prize vegetables, which they intended to submit to the Annual Horticultural Competition at Saturday's Village Fête.

The day passed happily. Later, the Sprite family re-hung the portrait of Mim. Dad drilled holes in the wall by the staircase and then screwed in special brackets. With Mum and Flame's help lifting, and with Grandma's steady hand on the stepladder, Dad placed the huge painting in its new home. As the sun went down over Sprite Towers, Sidney and Mim Sprite were reunited.

And later still, in her bedroom, Ash took out the magic

stone from her pocket and placed it on her bedside table, took off her jeans and bundled them up in a heap on her chair. She pulled on her pyjamas and climbed into bed. So busy had the day been, and so excited were the Sprite Sisters about the camp, that Ash had completely forgotten about the envelope in the back pocket of her jeans. When Mum came in to kiss her goodnight and picked up her clothes for the washing machine, Ash was tired and ready for sleep.

Ottalie Sprite walked down the wide mahogany staircase carrying a pile of her daughters' dirty socks, T-shirts and jeans and was about to walk through to the utility room, when the phone rang in the hallway. She put down the dirty clothes on the bottom stair and picked up the phone.

'Oh hi, Liz!' she said to her friend, and walked off to sit down in the drawing room and talk.

Upstairs, Ash was falling into a deep and dreamy sleep. But, as her mind and her body relaxed into slumber, the magic stone emitted a piercing squeak.

'What is it? What's happened?' she shouted, sitting up. She stared into the dark in a state of shock.

Beeeep! went the stone again. Ash jumped – turned to look at the stone, rubbed her eyes.

'I was asleep,' she said to the stone. 'Let me be.' And she began to lie down again.

Beeeep!

Ash dragged herself back up and stared at the stone, blearily.

'All right, all right,' she said. 'Keep your hair on.'

She climbed out of bed and stood in the middle of the room, the magic stone in her right hand. What is it, she wondered. What are you trying to tell me? Her mind began to turn slowly.

Then she remembered. The envelope. The envelope she put in her back pocket.

My jeans, she thought, spinning around – and saw the empty chair. Oh no – Mum's taken them for washing!

Now fully awake, Ash flung open her bedroom door and raced down the stairs. She could hear Mum talking in the drawing room – and there, on the bottom stair, was the pile of dirty clothes.

She heard her mother move back towards the door, saying, 'Okay Liz, well that would be great.'

Quick, quick, thought Ash, as she rummaged through the clothes, throwing things in all directions.

She snatched up her jeans and felt around the pockets.

There it was. The envelope! She grabbed the corner and pulled hard, threw the jeans on the floor, then ran as fast as she could up the wide mahogany staircase.

As Ash closed the door to her bedroom, Mum came out of the drawing room and saw the pile of clothes strewn all over the hallway floor.

I'm sure it wasn't like that a minute ago, thought Mum. She sighed, picked up the pile of jeans and T-shirts, walked through to the utility room and stuffed everything into the washing machine. One minute later, Ash's jeans were soaking wet.

CHAPTER TWO

THE CAMP BEGINS

MONDAY MORNING shone sunny and bright. Ash woke early and lay in her bed for a moment, thinking. She remembered the night before and the race to retrieve the envelope.

Where was it, she wondered and turned to look at the little table by the side of her bed. There it was, propped up.

The door burst open. Marina's head appeared around the door. 'Come on, Ash! We've got to get the camp started!' she said.

In a minute, Ash was washed and dressed. She grabbed the envelope and stuffed it into the back pocket of her clean pair of jeans.

Mustn't forget it this time, she thought, pushing the magic stone into her front pocket.

＊　＊　＊

After a quick breakfast, the Sprite Sisters raced down to the caravan.

'Okay, we've got to think about what we'll need,' said Flame, looking around.

'Sleeping bags,' said Marina.

'Teddy bears,' said Ariel.

'Cheese,' said Ash. 'Why do we need teddy bears?'

'Cos we just do,' said Ariel.

Within a few minutes, the Sprite Sisters ran back to the house.

Up and down, back and forth over the wide rolling lawn they went, all morning long, carrying sleeping bags, blankets, pillows, torches, books, bottles of water, a huge old frying pan, an old saucepan, an assortment of cutlery and cooking utensils, camping stools, clothes, food including lots of tins of baked beans, a washing-up bowl – everything they thought they would need.

Bert lolloped along for a bit, but he soon got bored and lay down on the terrace and went to sleep in a sausage-doggy heap.

'Can't I use my magic power to lift all this stuff down to the camp?' said Ariel, on one trip upstairs.

'It would save a lot of effort, but I think Mum might notice somehow,' said Marina. She looked at her little, blond-haired sister, carrying a great pile of soft toys. 'You don't have to take *all* your teddy bears, Ariel!'

The girls worked hard and by lunchtime the camp was ready.

Flame and Marina had dug a fire hole in the ground and

they had all helped to gather firewood from the Wild Woods. They laid bits of wood in the hole, to make the campfire. Flame lit it with her magic power of Fire and the first lot of 'Cheese Dreams' – fried cheese and chutney sandwiches – were cooked for lunch and eaten with great relish and much licking of fingers.

'The camp begins!' said Flame.

While the Sprite Sisters had been raiding the fridge and pantry and running to and fro that morning, Mum had been busy finding things for the bric-a-brac stall for the Village Fête on Saturday.

There were many cupboards at Sprite Towers. Several of these had been cleared out recently by Grandma and Mrs Duggery, the magical old lady who came to protect Sprite Towers against Glenda Glass – but there were still cupboards in the house that had remained untouched for many years.

Unlike her husband, Ottalie Sprite did not like clutter, so she was happy to send things for the bric-a-brac stall. It's all for a good cause, she thought.

Since Dad was at his office, that day was a good time to fill up some boxes and drop off the things at the Village Hall.

If Colin were at home, he'd wangle it all back into the house, thought Mum. So she seized the opportunity to clear one of the cupboards on the first floor of the house.

At the back of this, she found a number of portraits stacked up against the wall.

Nobody's been in here for years, thought Mum. It's lucky I looked. Charles Smythson can have a look at these when he comes. And she carried on searching for things to send to the fête.

One of the things Mum found was a small wooden box with a pattern on the lid. It was long enough to store pencils and wide enough to hold an envelope. It reminded her of those old-fashioned cigar boxes people used to have, when she was young.

The box was locked and Mum was unable to open it. To her, it didn't seem special. It looked like one of many similar things at Sprite Towers – so she lobbed it into her cardboard box.

After lunch, with Dad still out of the house, Grandma weeding the rose garden and her daughters down at their camp, Mum carried downstairs eight cardboard boxes full of old things and put them in the big red car. Then she drove them to the Village Hall, ready for Saturday's fete.

Later that afternoon, Mum and the Sprite Sisters went to collect Ash's new rabbit.

Fudge, Ash's little brown and white rabbit, had been killed when Glenda Glass attacked the house and a branch fell straight through the roof of his hutch. The girls had been very upset.

Soon after that, the whole family had driven to France for their summer holiday, to see their grandparents. Ottalie's mother was French and her father English, and they lived in the Dordogne in France. Every summer, the Sprites drove down to stay with them.

Now they were back home and it was time to collect the new rabbit.

When Ash held him up – a small ball of pale gold fluff and large black eyes – her sisters went all gooey.

'Oh, Mum,' pleaded Flame, Marina and Ariel. 'Can we each have a new rabbit?'

Mum shook her head. 'You have enough pets to look after,' she said. Ten guinea pigs, six rabbits, two gerbils, Bert the sausage dog, and Pudding, the large grey tabby cat, were quite enough, she maintained.

'What are you going to call him, Ash?' asked Mum.

'Peanut,' replied Ash, stroking him.

'Good name,' said Mum.

'*Please*, Mum!' the other three wailed.

'No, darlings – enjoy and value the things that you already have,' said Mum.

Dad was there when they got home and he, too, thought Peanut was very sweet.

Then Mum, Dad and Grandma sat on the terrace in the sunshine, with a bottle of wine, while the Sprite Sisters played on the lawn with some of their rabbits and guinea pigs.

'It's lovely to feel so relaxed,' said Dad, leaning back in his chair and looking around at the garden.

'What, after all that worry with the roof and Oswald trying to buy the house?' said Mum.

Dad nodded. 'I'm relieved that's all over, that Sprite Towers is safe – and that everything and everyone is okay.'

'Yes,' said Mum, taking his hand.

Grandma smiled. Perhaps it was because she and the girls knew that Glenda Glass was far away that they felt safe. Verena – Glenda's granddaughter and the girls' distant cousin – was gone too, to South America to see her mother. In her absence, the friendship between Flame and Marina had strengthened once more. Even Flame, alert and protective of her younger sisters, was relaxed.

As the Sprite family enjoyed the warm evening sunshine, everything felt wonderful. Everything felt perfect.

A little later, Dad and Ash went down to the vegetable garden to do the watering and check on their vegetables. With the horticultural show approaching, this was an important week for them and they planned to enter a number of classes.

Over by the stables, Marina and Ariel put fresh water in the hutches of their animals.

In the kitchen, Mum and Grandma prepared supper – homemade fish pie and salad from the garden – while Flame laid the table.

At the supper table that evening, there was an air of great excitement.

'Camping out tonight, girls, eh?' said Dad.

The Sprite Sisters' faces glowed with anticipation. After they had helped to clear the dishes, brushed their teeth and had a shower, they set off to the camp.

'Night!' they shouted, as they ran across the wide rolling lawn, down to the edge of the Wild Woods.

'I'll come and check up on you a little later,' shouted Dad, from the terrace. 'And remember the kitchen door is open – and you have your phones. Just shout if you need anything.'

'We won't need anything!' said Flame, stopping and turning. 'And you're not to come creeping around the caravan listening to our conversations! They're private!'

Dad burst out laughing. 'Righty-ho!' he chortled. 'Let's hope it doesn't rain. We don't yet know if the caravan is watertight.'

'Do you think they'll be all right?' asked Mum, beside him, as her daughters sped out of sight.

'Of course they'll be all right, love,' said Dad, putting his arm around her.

As the moon rose and the early August sky deepened to twilight blue, the Sprite Sisters lay in their sleeping bags and chattered in the dark.

Ariel was just telling them about Sidney Sprite, when Ash's magic stone gave out a mighty squeak – and Ash nearly fell off her bunk.

'Eeek!' she cried.

'What's the matter?' cried Flame, Marina and Ariel, sitting up in their sleeping bags. 'What's happened?'

'Did you hear it?' asked Ash, her face white.

'Hear what?' asked Flame.

'The magic stone squeaked!' said Ash.

'No, I didn't hear anything,' said Flame.

'Nor me,' said Marina.

Ariel pursed her lips and shook her head.

Ash frowned. 'I wonder why you didn't hear it . . . You've all heard it before . . .'

'I don't know – but what's it telling you?' asked Flame, drawing up her long legs and folding her arms around them.

Ash scrabbled out of her sleeping bag. 'Oh blimey, I keep forgetting,' she said. 'It's the envelope I found behind the painting. The stone is reminding me about it.'

'What envelope?' asked Ariel.

Ash stood up, grabbed her jeans and pulled out the envelope. Flame, Marina and Ariel climbed off their beds in their sleeping bags. They looked like huge caterpillars as they jumped towards Ash's bed and flopped down on it.

Flame held the torch steady, while Ash showed them the stiff white envelope. 'I found this behind Great-Great-Grandma Mim's portrait,' she explained.

'You didn't tell us!' said Flame.

'Well, we've all been so busy – and I kept forgetting,' said Ash. 'It's lucky I remembered it was in my jeans last night, otherwise we'd have lost it in the washing machine.'

'So, what is it and who is it from?' asked Marina, her brown eyes glowing.

'Hold it up – I can't see!' said Ariel.

Ash held up the envelope in the torchlight.

'*The Sprite Sisters, Sprite Towers*,' read Flame. She screwed up her face. 'Have there been other sets of Sprite Sisters apart from us?'

Marina, Ash and Ariel shrugged.

'Open it up, Ash,' said Flame. 'Here – use my Swiss Army knife, then you won't tear it. It looks very precious.'

'Thanks,' said Ash. Carefully, she slit open the envelope with the pocket knife.

'Come on, hurry up!' said Marina.

The four Sprite Sisters held their breath as Ash pulled out the letter.

There were two small sheets of paper, folded in half. The

ink was black, the handwriting was elegant and rather old-fashioned in style – and covered the front of both sheets of paper.

At the top right-hand side of the letter was the address.

It read, *Sprite Towers*. Then underneath was written the date, *6th June 1917*.

'Oh my goodness!' said Ash. 'Look!'

She held up the letter for her sisters to see clearly.

'*Dear Flame, Marina, Ash and Ariel,*' read Ariel. 'That's *us*!'

Flame, Marina, Ash and Ariel looked at one another in amazement.

'This letter was written nearly a century ago,' said Flame, almost in a whisper. 'It's spooky.'

They were silent for a moment. Then Marina said, 'See who it's from.'

Ash turned over to the second page. At the bottom of this, the letter was signed, *Yours, George Sprite*.

'Who's George Sprite?' said Marina. 'Have Mum and Dad or Grandma ever mentioned him?'

'Not that I remember,' said Flame. 'This is really weird.'

'You don't think Dad could have hidden the letter behind Mim's portrait as a joke to fool us?' said Marina.

'Why would he have done that?' asked Ash.

'I dunno – it's just a thought,' shrugged Marina.

'Flame, you read it out,' said Ash, handing the letter to her. 'I'll hold the torch.'

'Okay,' said Flame.

They shuffled along the bunk until they were all comfortable.

'Okay, here goes,' and Flame read:

'*Dear Flame, Marina, Ash and Ariel,*

I will be leaving shortly to go back to fight at the Front and I know that I may never return. I am nineteen years old this month.'

'What's the Front?' asked Ariel. 'Why was he fighting?'

'1917 was the First World War,' explained Flame. 'The Front was the line where the armies met in France and Belgium. All the young men had to go and fight there – that was where the battles were. George might have been injured and come home on leave, but he must have had to go back again.'

'I wonder what happened to him,' said Ariel.

Flame sighed sadly. 'I don't think he would have left this letter here if he had come back.'

Then she read on: '*There is much magic in this house and it must be guarded carefully. People have already tried to get it, but so far Father and I have stopped them.*'

Flame stopped, her face thoughtful. Then she said, 'He must mean Sidney Sprite. If this was written in 1917 and George was a young man, it means he's probably one of Sidney's sons.'

'Could he be our great-grandfather?' asked Ash.

'Not if he didn't come back,' said Flame, biting her lip. She took a deep breath, then continued:

'*In case I do not come home, I have hidden this letter and I know you will find it. In the envelope is also a key.*'

'Is there a key, Ash?' said Flame. She took the torch as Ash peered into the thick white envelope.

'Yes, there's a little key right down in the corner.' She pulled it out and held it up in the torchlight.

'That looks like the key for a small box,' said Flame.

'What does George say next?' asked Marina.

'*There is a box that you must find,*' read Flame. '*I left it hidden in a cupboard in my room, but it may have been moved by the time you read this. You must find the box to unlock the secret of the towers. It is a small wooden box, the size of a cigar box. On the lid is painted a crossed circle.*'

Ash gasped. 'That's what Mrs Duggery said we had to look for – the crossed circle!'

'Yes, you're right – she did,' agreed Flame. She bit her lip again, thinking about this, then read on. '*In the box is something very precious. Guard it with your life. If you discover the power of the house, we may meet one day. Yours, George Sprite.*'

Flame stared at the letter. 'This is . . . this is . . . all very strange,' she said, quietly.

'Do you think George *did* come back?' said Ariel.

'No, pumpkin, I don't think he came back to Sprite Towers,' said Flame. 'I have a feeling he was killed in the Great War.'

'Oh, poor George!' said Ariel. Marina put her arm around her little sister and held her close.

For a moment, they were silent, each touched by a sense of sadness. Tears trickled down their faces.

Just then, there was a sharp rap on the door. They all jumped, as Dad shouted, 'Everything all right, girls?'

'Blimey, you nearly gave us a heart attack, Dad!' shouted Flame. 'Yes, we're all fine!'

'Well, don't forget the kitchen door's open – and lock your door from the inside. Sleep well!'

'Night, Dad,' they all shouted back. And off Dad went through the dark.

Flame, Marina and Ariel hobbled back to their bunks. When they were settled down, Flame turned off the torch and they lay there in the darkness. Outside, the moon rose over the trees.

'Poor George,' said Ariel, yawning. Then she turned over and fell asleep.

'Which do you suppose was his bedroom at Sprite Towers?' whispered Ash.

'I don't know,' Flame whispered back. 'We need to find out who George is. If he was living at home, he was probably unmarried. Maybe Grandma will know – we should ask her in the morning, before she leaves to go and dog-sit for her friend, Valerie.'

'Perhaps this Charles person will know,' said Marina.

'Yes, we could ask him,' said Flame. At the mention of Charles Smythson, Ash's stone squeaked. 'Did you hear that?' she asked.

'What?' whispered Flame and Marina.

'The magic stone – it squeaked!' hissed Ash.

'No, I didn't hear it,' whispered Flame.

'Nor me,' said Marina.

'How strange,' whispered Ash. 'It keeps squeaking. When Dad mentioned that man – it squeaked then, at the table, but no one else seemed to hear it.'

'Do you think it's warning us?' asked Marina.

'Could be.'

'Well, we mustn't alert Charles to our magic powers,'

whispered Flame. 'We've got to find out about George without sounding as if we're asking anything in particular.'

'And we've got to search for the box,' Ash added.

'Sprite Towers is so full of stuff it's difficult to know where to start,' whispered Marina, yawning.

'Maybe the stone will guide us,' said Ash.

For a while they were silent. Flame lay on her back, her hands under her head, staring into the dark. She was just about to ask her sisters another question, when she realised they were both sound asleep.

What does the letter mean, wondered Flame. What is the secret of the towers? I wonder who was trying to get at the magic in the house. Maybe it was one of the Sprites whose magic went bad?

Flame lay there for another few minutes, thinking about this. Outside in the Wild Woods, an owl hooted. Close by, a fox barked. Around the old white caravan, the tall pine trees rustled in the night breeze.

There's magic in the towers, thought Flame, and we have to guard it with our lives . . .

And with that she fell asleep.

CHAPTER THREE

THE
CAMPFIRE

'BREAKFAST!' SHOUTED Ariel, running out to the campfire.

'I'll go and get some bacon and eggs from the kitchen,' said Ash, dashing off.

'I'll light the fire,' said Flame.

For the next five minutes, she and Ariel built up the fire, using kindling and branches they had collected from the Wild Woods the day before. Then Flame pointed her finger, used her magic power of Fire – and whoosh, in an instant the campfire was burning nicely.

Meanwhile, Marina tidied up then used her magic power of water to put clean water into their drinking bottles. 'Hey, I'm getting good at this magic stuff,' she said.

A minute later, Ash appeared with a basket of bacon and

eggs. Seeing Marina using her magic power to create fresh orange juice for their breakfast, she laughed and said, 'What would Grandma say about us using your power for things like this? She's always told us we're only to use our powers wisely and for good!'

Flame turned to her, a thoughtful look on her face. 'I don't think she'd mind. We're not hurting anyone and it's not an *unwise* use of our power.'

'You reckon?' asked Ash, considering this thought.

Marina piped in. 'In some ways, it's a good chance for us to practise our magic,' she said.

Ash grinned suddenly. 'Well, in that case, perhaps you can wash up the plates from yesterday's lunch! We seem to have forgotten about those!'

Marina laughed and set about honing her magic skills until the plates and cutlery gleamed like new.

The Sprite Sisters got on with the cooking. Flame put some oil into the frying pan, while Ariel cut slices of Mum's homemade bread on a wooden board.

A little while later, they sat on their stools around the fire, munching. Bert sat beside them, hopeful for a piece of food.

'It doesn't look like it does when Mum or Grandma cooks it,' giggled Ariel, prodding the jumbled mix of charred fried eggs and bacon on her plate.

'But it tastes every bit as good,' said Ash, tucking in.

'Yes, it has that authentic campfire flavour!' said Marina and they all laughed.

'So what's the plan today?' asked Flame, although this wasn't so much a question, as an indication that she was about to tell them what they'd do. Flame was the organiser – and she was good at it, though it sometimes rankled with Marina, who was more of a free spirit and liked to do something if and when she felt like it. Ash usually agreed with Flame's plans and Ariel lived in her own little dream world, so she often didn't notice that she was being organised anyway.

As her sisters chomped through mouthfuls of breakfast, Flame answered her own question. 'Well, first we must go and say goodbye to Grandma and ask her about George's box. After that, I think we ought to start the hunt.' She turned to her sisters, and asked, 'What do you think?'

'Yes,' they agreed, nodding their heads.

'So where should we begin searching?' asked Marina.

To this, even Flame was silent. Where *should* they start? Sprite Towers was a massive house with four floors, attics, ten bedrooms and several dozen cupboards.

A minute later they had finished eating and put down their plates on the grass. Bert stared at the discarded plates, and, thinking no one was watching, began to pick off the pieces of uneaten bacon – until Flame saw him and swooshed him away. 'Get off, Bert!' she said.

'I think we should look in George's bedroom,' said Ash, as she picked up the plates from the ground.

'But we don't know which room was his bedroom,' said Marina. 'I think we should start in the attics.'

'Why do you think the box would be in the attics?' asked Ariel, collecting up the tomato sauce bottle and empty glasses.

'We've got to start somewhere,' shrugged Marina. 'There's lots of junk up there.'

As Flame damped down the campfire, she called over, 'Let's start in the towers and work down through the attics.'

'Okay,' the others agreed.

Then Flame said, 'Let's think about this. I've the power of Fire and I can burn and heat things. Marina, your power of Water means you can create rivers, make ice or take all the fluid out of something. Ash, you've the power of Earth and can bind things to the ground, so that they can't move. And Ariel, your power of Air allows you to lift things and create great winds to blow them away.' She stopped for a second, then said, 'But which of us can *find* things? That's a good question.'

'Do you remember, I found the gerbils when they got lost,' said Ash. 'But this feels different.' She reached into her jeans pocket. 'Hey, I know what we should do,' she said. 'We'll use the stone! I'm sure it will guide us. We could ask it, *Am I getting nearer or further away?* – like the hot and cold game.'

'Good idea,' her sisters agreed.

'Okay, well we'd better clear up before we start the search,' said Flame, and for the next half hour they washed up and tidied up until the camp looked shipshape. Then they ran over the lawn to the house.

'Go and clean your teeth, girls,' said Mum, as they burst in through the kitchen door.

'Oh, Mu-uum!' they groaned, then pounded up the stairs to their bedrooms.

A little while later, the clean Sprite Sisters came downstairs. Mum and Grandma were standing in the hallway.

'Come and say goodbye to your grandmother, girls,' said Mum.

'I didn't realise you were leaving so soon, Grandma!' said Flame, coming up to the tall, elegant woman with the strawberry-blond bob.

'Why, love – is there something you want to ask me?' said Grandma – but knew, instantly, from Flame's expression that whatever it was she could not mention it with her mother close by.

'When are you back?' asked Flame.

'Probably Friday – it just depends on when Valerie gets back,' said Grandma. 'Will it keep till then?'

'Yes,' smiled Flame and hugged her grandmother close.

Then Marina, Ash and Ariel hugged her too. The Sprite Sisters loved their grandmother. She knew about their magic powers and was their guide and mentor. Marilyn Sprite had once had the power herself, many years ago, before she had lost it in a battle with Glenda Glass. And recently it had seemed that it might be returning . . .

Now she smiled proudly at her granddaughters, then turned to give Ottalie a kiss. A minute later they had waved her off.

As Mum closed the huge front door, the Sprite Sisters ran up the stairs to the attics and made their way along the corridor to the West Tower. They opened the small latched wooden door and climbed the rickety spiral stairs that led up to the tower.

Then there they were, standing in the West Tower – a large, round, empty room with a wooden floor. Above them was a dome of glass: it was here that Sidney Sprite had kept his telescope and studied the stars. Since the roof had been repaired, Mum and Dad allowed the girls to go up to the towers once more.

Ash got out her magic stone and asked if they were close to George's box. Was it, perhaps, hidden in the wall here? The stone lay silent in the palm of her hand.

'Okay, East Tower,' said Flame and they pounded along the attic corridor to the other tower. There they opened another small latched door and climbed a second rickety spiral staircase.

This room had a high ceiling and arched windows that afforded a view of the countryside in every direction. For a few moments, the Sprite Sisters gazed out over the fields. Beyond the grounds of Sprite Towers to the east, were fields of stubble where the winter barley had been harvested the week before. To the west, they could see a huge yellow combine harvester moving slowly along a field of golden-ripe wheat. 'Look, they're harvesting over there,' said Flame.

Beyond the fields were woods and the river, wending its way through the gently undulating landscape of north Norfolk. Above it all was the huge sky.

'What a lovely view!' exclaimed Ash.

A moment later their thoughts turned to the hunt for the magic box.

The magic stone was silent, however. 'It's not here either,' said Flame. 'Let's go down to the attics.'

Back the Sprite Sisters went and worked their way along the attics, room by room.

'This is where I thought it would be,' said Marina. 'There's so much stuff up here – it could easily have got hidden.'

But still the stone was silent. Next, they went down to the second floor of the house and worked their way through their own bedrooms, the small guest room and various cupboards. Still nothing.

'It must be somewhere downstairs,' said Flame.

So the Sprite Sisters went down to the first floor. Here were their parents' bedroom and their grandmother's bedroom and sitting room, along with the big guest room, the second guest room and more cupboards. They went from room to room, but still the stone was silent in Ash's hand.

They stood together on the first-floor landing, looking down to the hallway. 'What do we do now?' asked Ash.

'How about Ariel asks Sidney – see if he knows,' suggested Flame.

'Okay,' agreed Ariel. They ran down to the bottom of the wide mahogany staircase.

'Hang on, Ariel – where are Mum and Dad?' asked Marina.

'Dad's at the office and I think Mum's in the kitchen,' said Flame.

They all waited for a second just to be sure, then Ariel began to chat to Sidney Sprite's portrait. Flame, Marina and Ash crowded around her.

After a few seconds, she turned to her sisters and said, 'He doesn't think the box is here. He says he asked us to move Mim's portrait so we would find George's letter, but he thinks the box is no longer in the house. He says he's very happy to have Mim beside him again though.'

'Oh – well, tell him we're very happy for him,' said Flame.

Once again, Ariel spoke quietly to her great-great-grandfather. The Sprite Sisters were so engrossed, they did not hear Mum come out of the kitchen and walk through to the hallway.

'What are you doing?' Her voice rang out behind them. The Sprite Sisters spun around.

'Oh, er – we were – er, Ariel was talking to Sidney,' said Flame. 'He says he's happy Mim is beside him.'

'Riiight,' said Mum, slowly.

'What time is this Charles man coming, Mum?' asked Ariel. She was very good at distracting people when things got tricky.

'About four o'clock – and Dad will be back by then,' replied Mum. 'We'll all have supper together this evening.'

'Okay,' the girls replied. 'We're going back to the camp now. See you later.'

Bert's barking alerted the Sprite Sisters to Charles Smythson's arrival. The Sprite Sisters had been having cycling races around the lawn, in and out of various obstacles they placed on the grass, when a silver car came up the drive and stopped at the front of the house.

As Charles got out, Mum and Dad walked to greet him and the Sprite Sisters whizzed around the corner on their bikes.

'Welcome to Sprite Towers!' said Dad, shaking Charles's hand.

'Thank you, Colin!' said Charles, smiling.

The Sprite Sisters were dazzled – everyone was dazzled. Charles Smythson was so handsome he looked as if he'd stepped off the pages of a magazine.

They all walked around to the terrace. Drinks were

fetched and for the next hour they all sat and talked.

Charles was witty and intelligent and interesting. Tall, dark-haired, dark-eyed, utterly charming and twenty-eight years old, he seemed to be perfect. Even his teeth were perfect.

Every time Charles smiled at Flame, she blushed a deep crimson. It was torture. Marina blushed too. Ash smiled and Ariel giggled.

Mum and Dad and Charles rattled on together about art and architecture, history and the Sprite family. Flame and Marina joined in, too. The younger Sprite Sisters mostly listened.

Then Charles turned to the girls and said, 'You are an interesting lot of sisters.'

'How do you mean?' asked Flame, wondering if he could somehow see their magical powers.

'Well, you all look completely different from each other!' said Charles, smiling. 'You have straight copper-colour hair and green eyes, Flame. Marina, you've got dark curly hair and blue eyes.' He turned to Ash. 'And you've thick chestnut brown hair and brown eyes. And Ariel . . . ' He smiled down at her. 'Ariel has wavy blond hair and grey eyes.'

'I look like Grandma,' said Flame. 'You'll see, when she comes back.'

'And I look like Dad,' said Ash, proudly.

'Yes, you do,' agreed Charles.

'And Ariel looks like me,' said Mum, putting her arm around her youngest daughter.

'True,' agreed Charles. 'And Marina?' He grinned at her.

'Marina looks like her grandfather, Sheldon Sprite,' said

Mum. 'You'll see it on the portraits.'

'Ah, yes, of course!' said Charles – and they laughed. Then he said, 'Well, you girls must tell me all about yourselves.'

Flame, Marina and Ash tensed in their seats at this request, but Ariel blurted out, 'We've got a camp and a campfire!'

'But you're not to come there,' said Flame, quickly. 'No grown-ups are allowed. Not unless they are invited.'

'Well, perhaps you will invite me,' said Charles with a charming smile. 'I should love to see your camp.'

'You can all come down tomorrow and we'll cook you supper on the campfire,' said Ariel. 'We can ask you about —'

Flame, Marina and Ash started. Oh no, they thought. What is Ariel going to say now? For a moment, they held their breath. Then Dad said, 'So how is Stephen?'

The girls breathed out, as Charles turned to Dad and smiled. 'He's well, I think. I am very grateful to him for all his help – he's been terrific.'

'Yes, he's a good chap,' agreed Dad, leaning over to fill up Charles's wine glass. 'Do you see a lot of him in London?'

'Thank you – no, not a lot,' said Charles.

'What's your relationship to Stephen?' asked Mum.

'He's my first cousin,' replied Charles.

'On whose side?' asked Mum, offering him a cheese nibble.

'On my father, Bernard's, side,' said Charles. 'His elder sister is Stephen's mother.'

Dad broke in, 'How are your parents?' he asked. 'Long time since I've seen them.'

'They're both well, thank you,' replied Charles, smiling.

'Are they still living in London?'

'No, they moved to Dorset when my father retired a few years ago,' said Charles.

'Ah yes, I think Stephen had told me that,' said Dad, nodding.

Mum lifted her hand in the air. 'Hang on a mo, chaps – just come back to the cousins. So is Glenda Glass your aunt, Charles?'

'Yes,' nodded Charles, taking a sip of wine.

Mum held Charles's gaze for a second. She didn't know anything about Glenda's Glass's magic, but she did not like the woman. Recently Grandma had found out that Glenda was probably the person who had defrauded her and run off with the family inheritance.

The Sprite Sisters glanced at their mother, then at Charles – and waited.

Then Mum asked, 'Do you see much of your Aunt Glenda?'

'No,' said Charles. 'I haven't seen her for years. My father and she were never close – and I believe she has lived abroad most of her life.'

'So how do you know Stephen so well?'

'I haven't known him well, but I am now getting to know him better,' replied Charles. 'Our families rarely got together when I was a child and Stephen is quite a few years older than me, so our paths didn't cross. As you know, though, he's a well-known patron of the Arts. I thought he might be able to help me get started professionally, so when I completed my doctoral thesis on eighteenth-century portraits in Devon country houses last year, I got in touch with him. Stephen very kindly commissioned me to do an inventory of his paintings – he's got a big collection. And that led me here, to Sprite Towers. It turned out Stephen is interested in the family history and was keen for you all to have an inventory of the portraits of the different branches of the Sprite family.'

'Yes, it's a good idea,' said Dad.

'So you're a Sprite, too,' said Flame, looking at him with her clear green eyes.

Charles turned and smiled at her. 'Yes, I'm a Sprite.'

'Are you related to Sidney Sprite?' asked Ariel.

Charles smiled again. 'My great-grandmother was Sidney Sprite's older sister, Margaret,' he said.

Just as he said this, Ash's magic stone squeaked. *Beeeep!* it went in her pocket. She sat up with a start, gasped and looked around the table. Had anyone else heard it, she wondered. She thought Charles glanced around at her – she was sitting at the far end of the table – but couldn't be sure. She'd been looking at her sisters – was expecting them to react and turn to her. But *they* were looking at Charles and did not seem to have heard the stone.

How strange, thought Ash, reaching for the stone in her pocket and feeling its smoothness. Had Charles glanced at her as the stone squeaked – or was she imagining it? Why – yet again – hadn't her sisters heard it?

Then Mum broke in, 'Colin, why don't you show Charles around while the girls and I get the supper ready.'

'Good idea,' said Dad. As they got up and went into the house, he turned to Charles and said, 'You're one of the family – so make yourself at home.'

* * *

40

Supper was delicious and entertaining. Everyone was on great form. The conversation flowed and the food went down a treat.

There was only one hiccup for the Sprite Sisters – when Mum related to Charles and Dad how she had found Ariel talking to Sidney Sprite and her sisters listening that morning. 'It was very amusing,' laughed Mum.

At this, Charles turned and looked at Ariel intently. Then he said, 'You must tell me all about your conversations with Sidney – I want to know everything.'

Ariel sat like a startled rabbit, fixed in the beam of Charles's dazzling smile – and nodded.

Flame, Marina and Ash looked at each other in alarm. They had to get Ariel out before anything else was said – and they must warn her.

'We've got to go back to the camp!' said Flame, standing up.

'But we haven't had cheese yet!' said Mum, surprised.

'We don't want cheese, thanks Mum,' said Flame. 'It'll keep us awake. It's getting dark. Come on, Ariel!'

'Oh – okay,' said Mum.

Flame yanked Ariel out of her chair and prodded her in the back. 'Say goodnight, Ariel!' she said.

The Sprite Sisters kissed their mother and father and waved shyly at Charles. 'Night, Charles,' they said.

'Night, girls! See you tomorrow!' he replied.

'I'll come down and check on you in a while,' said Dad. 'Inky night out there tonight – waning moon and it's behind the clouds. Hope you'll be able to see where you're going.'

'We're fine, Dad – really,' said Ash. 'We've got good torches.'

'I know, but I will come down otherwise your mother will worry,' laughed Dad.

The Sprite Sisters opened the kitchen door and went out into the dark.

As soon as they were tucked up in their sleeping bags in the caravan, the sisters began to chatter about Charles. Flame put the torch on its end in the middle of the floor, so they had a little light.

'He's so handsome!' said Marina.

'And so funny!' said Ariel.

'And very intelligent,' commented Flame.

'And interesting,' added Ash.

They were silent for a moment, then Ash said, 'My stone squeaked – did you hear it?'

'No, when?' her sisters asked her.

'I think it was when Charles said he was a Sprite.'

'What do you think it was trying to tell us?' asked Flame.

'I don't know,' replied Ash. 'Maybe we should be careful what we tell Charles.'

'Yes,' agreed Flame. 'Ariel you must be very careful what you tell *anyone* – including Charles – about your conversations with Sidney Sprite.'

'Why?' said Ariel, sitting up in her sleeping bag.

'For heaven's sake, Ariel!' said Flame, also sitting up. 'You know what Grandma has always told us: that we must keep our magic powers secret. *That's* why!'

'Do you think Charles has magic powers?' asked Ariel. 'He's a Sprite.'

'I doubt it,' replied Flame. 'Very few Sprites do have the power. Grandma says it skips whole generations.'

'We *must* find the magic box,' said Ash. 'George said that was the way to unlock the secret of the towers.'

'Yes,' they all agreed.

'And *quickly*,' added Flame. 'We have our Aussie cousins arriving at the end of next week and we won't have a moment to ourselves once they're here.'

'Maybe we need to strengthen our powers to find it,' suggested Ash.

'That's what Mrs Duggery said, didn't she,' said Marina, yawning. 'You know – about all working together and using our unique powers – Fire, Water, Earth and Air.'

Outside, in the pitch dark, Dad startled the girls for the second night running. 'Everything all right, girls?' he shouted, as he knocked on the door. 'Have you locked the door from the inside?'

'Yes, Dad – night!' they all called back.

'Okay, see you in the morning,' he called. And off he went back to the house.

One by one, the Sprite Sisters fell asleep. First Ariel, then Marina, then Ash.

Flame lay on her back, thinking about George and the box and Charles. Suddenly there seemed to be so many things to think about.

Eventually, as the wind rustled through the tall pine trees, she fell asleep.

CHAPTER FOUR

CHARLES
INVESTIGATES

THE SPRITE Sisters slept in a little later on Wednesday.

Outside the caravan, the grass was dewy. Big clouds swooshed across the sky and the air felt fresh.

Over breakfast, sitting on their stools around the campfire, the girls talked about the hunt for George's box and how they should proceed. Yesterday's search in the house had yielded nothing. Maybe the box was outside somewhere – in the stables, perhaps – but Ash's stone remained quiet.

'What do we do now?' asked Ariel.

'We can't stop looking,' said Flame. 'We *have* to find that box.'

'Let's read George's letter again,' suggested Marina.

Ash went into the caravan and retrieved the letter, which she had hidden beneath her mattress. She opened it and read it out, as her sisters listened, a look of deep seriousness on their faces.

'This is really important,' said Flame. 'George talks about guarding this secret with our *lives*. What on earth can it be?'

'We guarded Sprite Towers with our lives a few weeks ago, when Glenda Glass attacked the house,' said Marina. 'I can't imagine how things could get worse than that.'

'That was horrible,' said Ariel.

'Glenda Glass is away at the moment and Sprite Towers is safe,' said Flame, keen to reassure her younger sisters. 'Dad found a way to pay for the roof to be mended – and we won't have to leave Sprite Towers. But, yes, we do need to find out what George is trying to tell us.'

For a few seconds they were silent. Then Marina said, 'George says he left the box hidden in his room, but that it may have been moved by now. We don't know which was his room, but anyway the stone says the box isn't in the house. If it's not in the house, then where would it be that we can still find it?'

'I wonder what "no longer" means?' asked Flame. 'When Sidney told Ariel the box was "no longer" in the house, did he mean it was taken out a long time ago – or more recently? Grandma and Mrs Duggery had that big clear-out of some of the attic cupboards a few weeks ago.'

'So we know the box is probably not here, but not how or why it was taken out,' said Marina.

They were silent again, then Flame said, 'I think if we find out about George Sprite, we'll have a clearer idea. We'd be able to start building a picture.'

'Should we wait till Grandma gets back on Friday and ask her?' suggested Ash.

Flame shook her head. 'It won't leave us enough time – we need to get on with it before the Aussies arrive. Let's start by asking Charles. We don't have to tell him anything about the letter. I can say we're going to do a project on the First World War at school.'

The others agreed, then Marina added, 'I think we should keep looking for the box in the house – just in case.'

'Okay,' they all agreed.

By the time they had finished breakfast and cleared up the camp, Charles Smythson had arrived. Mum and Dad were sitting with him in the drawing room, showing him letters and documents they had that related to the Sprite family portraits. The Sprite Sisters sat on the arms of the big cream sofas and listened as Charles explained how he would do his research for the inventory.

'I'll start by looking at all the portraits in the house, to get an overall feel for the collection,' he explained. 'Then I'll measure the portraits and make detailed notes of the sitter and how it was painted – whether it's oils or watercolours, on canvas or on board. Then I will go around the collection again with a torch and magnifying glass to make a closer inspection of the paintwork.'

'What does that tell you?' asked Flame.

'It allows me to see if the painting has been added to or if anything has been covered up,' replied Charles. 'Sometimes you find another image underneath.'

'Ah right,' said Flame. 'And after that?'

'Well, *then* I take a photograph of everything,' replied

Charles. 'I'll be carrying about special lights and reflective silver umbrellas at that point.'

'What do the umbrellas do?' asked Marina.

'They diffuse the lights and ensure the paintings are evenly lit,' explained Charles. 'What you don't want is something called flare – bright spots of light on the painting.'

'And then that's it?' asked Flame.

'No, that's only half of it!' said Charles. He smiled around at the Sprite family. 'When I've got the information and photographs from Sprite Towers, I then go to London to piece all the research together.'

'Well, it'll be a busy time, but we will do our best,' said Mum. 'Obviously we'd appreciate it if you could get everything finished here by the end of next week, as Colin's sister and her family are coming over from Australia to stay with us.'

'Of course,' said Charles. 'I shall work as fast as possible.'

'It's exciting,' said Dad, getting up. 'It will be wonderful to have an inventory of all the paintings and to know what's what and who's who.'

Then Dad left to go to his office in town and Mum went off to give a piano lesson in the dining room. Charles walked up to the top of the house, followed by the Sprite Sisters.

'I'm not used to having an entourage,' he laughed.

'Well, we're really interested in what you're doing,' said Flame.

The girls watched and waited as Charles began to make notes in a small black book on the paintings up the staircase. Sometimes, he took a digital voice recorder out of his pocket and spoke into that, too.

The Sprite Sisters asked lots of questions. 'Who's this?' and 'What's that?' and 'When was that painted?'

Charles answered all their questions graciously.

'Are there any portraits painted around the time of the First World War?' asked Flame.

'Yes, there are several,' replied Charles. 'Why?'

'We're doing a project on the Great War next term and we've been asked to find out about people in our families who were in it,' said Flame.

'Well, how about you let me get on alone, now, so I can concentrate, and I'll let you know later which portraits there are from that time,' suggested Charles.

'Okay,' said Flame.

The Sprite Sisters ran down the garden to the swings that were attached to the tall lime tree at the east side of the garden. Two huge black tyres hung, suspended on thick ropes that had been tied around the high branches.

The girls took it in turns to swing, then moseyed off to play with their guinea pigs and rabbits on the lawn.

'Do you think he suspects anything?' asked Marina, lolling on the lawn.

'No, I don't think so,' replied Flame.

A little later, the sisters went back into the house to do another search for George's box.

Charles was still standing on the first-floor staircase, when they charged up to the attics once more. He was there a little later, when they came down again.

'What are you looking for?' he asked, casually, as they passed him.

'Oh, we're not looking for anything,' said Flame, 'We're just playing a game.'

Charles looked at Flame – and at that very moment, Ash's magic stone squeaked.

Beeep! it went. Flame, Marina and Ariel did not seem to have heard it – but Charles did.

He looked at Ash. She looked at him.

He heard it, she thought. *He heard my stone squeak!*

Ash put her hand in her pocket and felt the smooth shape of the magic stone. Quickly, she looked around again. Charles was still watching her. As their eyes met, she glanced away, confused. She drew a sharp breath, then said, suddenly, 'Come on, let's go back to the camp!' – and ran off down the stairs.

Flame, Marina and Ariel stared at their sister in surprise – then raced down the stairs and followed her over the lawn.

'What was all that about?' asked Flame, as soon as she caught up with her.

'He heard my stone squeak!' said Ash.

'When?' asked Marina.

'On the staircase – when he asked Flame what we were looking for,' said Ash, pulling the stone out of her pocket. 'I can't believe you didn't hear it!'

Flame, Marina and Ariel glanced at one another, silent. Ash stared, anxiously, at the stone lying in the palm of her hand. 'I wonder why Charles could hear it and not you?' she said. 'It's so strange.'

Marina put a reassuring hand on Ash's shoulder. 'Listen,

he might have heard a squeaking noise, but he wouldn't know it was your magic stone,' she said. 'I mean not many people carry magic squeaking stones about in their pockets, do they!'

'He definitely heard it,' said Ash, her brown eyes wide with anxiety. 'He looked straight at me. I could feel his eyes boring into me!'

'Yes, but he won't know what the noise was, silly!' laughed Marina. 'He'll probably think it was a text coming through on someone's mobile.'

Mum had insisted that, if the girls were to have supper down at the camp that evening, they should eat a proper lunch at the house, so at one o'clock, Mum, Charles and the girls sat around the kitchen table. Ash felt awkward, but Charles appeared to have completely forgotten about the squeaking noise and was easy and relaxed. He complimented Mum on the delicious meal of homemade steak and mushroom pie and homegrown vegetables, then turned to the Sprite Sisters.

'So, supper at the camp this evening then!' he said, with a dazzling smile. 'What's on the menu?'

'Sausages,' replied Ariel, grinning.

'That's good – I love sausages!' said Charles.

Then he turned to Flame and said, 'I'll show you the First World War portraits as soon as I find them.'

'Thank you,' smiled Flame.

'What's this, Flame?' asked Mum.

'I was asking Charles about portraits from the First World War,' said Flame. 'We're doing a project on it next term and I wondered which Sprites had fought in it.'

'That's interesting,' said Mum. 'Well, I'm sure Charles will be able to help. He's the expert.'

'Yes, I'd be very pleased to,' said Charles, his white teeth gleaming.

'And of course, Flame, your grandmother knows quite a bit about the family history,' added Mum. 'You can ask her when she gets back.'

Flame sighed quietly. Friday was a long way away. We must find George Sprite before then, she thought.

As if catching her thoughts, Charles Smythson glanced over at her and said, 'I'm sure it won't take me long to find them.'

'Thank you,' repeated Flame politely.

Charles looked over at the eldest Sprite Sister, then asked casually, 'Is there a particular portrait you are looking for?'

Flame shook her head – though she knew this would look unconvincing. She found it very difficult to tell fibs and her face always gave her away.

'George!' blurted out Ariel. 'We're looking for George!'

Flame spun around to her sister. 'Ariel!' she hissed, aghast.

Charles watched, bemused, as Marina and Ash gave their little sister furious looks.

Marina caught Flame's eye – as if to tell her she was trying to rescue the situation – then said, jokingly, to Charles, 'Flame's got this thing about a boy called George!'

'I thought it was Quinn you liked, Flame,' said Mum, grinning. 'You are a dark horse!'

Flame blushed a deep crimson. This is getting worse every second, she thought, and felt herself sliding down under the table. At the same time, she gave Ariel a look like thunder.

'Flame always goes like this when you mention the name George,' said Ariel.

'*I do not!*' hissed Flame, sitting up straight very quickly and stabbing a piece of carrot with her fork.

'Ariel, shut up!' said Marina.

'Well, I shall be on the lookout for a man called George!' laughed Charles, as he took another potato from the dish.

Ariel got a thorough telling off from her sisters that afternoon, and had to promise them she would not mention George Sprite again to Charles Smythson.

By seven o' clock that evening, things were harmonious once more, as Mum, Dad and Charles made their down to the camp. Beside them, Bert lolloped along, his big ears flapping.

'You are officially invited in,' said Ariel, holding open the rope gate.

'Thank you!' laughed Mum. 'We're honoured.'

'Absolutely!' added Dad.

'Please sit down on the stools,' said Marina, pointing.

Mum, Dad and Charles settled in front of the blazing fire.

'Quite a fire you've got there, this evening,' commented Dad. 'Might be a bit hot for cooking. Do you want me to help you calm it down?'

'Be quiet, Dad!' said Flame. 'We're in charge.'

Dad made a silly face and said, 'Okay, chef.'

Ariel handed out plates and cutlery, while Marina offered them bread rolls. Ash poured out glasses of Mum's home-made elderflower cordial and Flame wrestled with the sausages in the huge frying pan.

Mum watched her elder daughter, wondering whether to say anything about cooking the sausages more slowly, so that they cooked evenly – but decided to keep quiet.

Charles smiled. 'This is such fun!' he said, holding his plate in front of him.

A few minutes later, Flame lifted the piping-hot frying pan off the fire and laid it on the grass. The sausages – which started life large and plump – had shrivelled to crusty, black lumps.

Flame was hot and red-faced. She pushed back her hair from her face, then lifted up the pan for Marina to serve out the sausages.

'Well done, girls!' said Mum and Dad, trying not to laugh.

They all stabbed at their sausages, but the charred objects were so hard they couldn't get their forks into them. Mum's sausage shot off the plate – and was quickly caught and eaten by an eager Bert.

Charles's sausage splatted his cashmere sweater, then dropped on to his linen trousers. He picked it off and smiled politely.

Dad managed to cut his sausage open, only to find that the inside was almost raw. He rubbed his hand over his chin, a sure sign that he wasn't quite sure what to do.

Thankfully, Flame burst out laughing – and they all laughed.

'It was a good first attempt!' said Mum. 'Why don't we go back to the house and I'll rustle up some omelettes.'

They gathered up their things and walked back to the house, leaving Bert happily eating the abandoned sausages. Sausage was sausage, after all.

CHAPTER FIVE

CHARLES SMYTHSON was in a good mood when he left The Oaks on Thursday morning. He'd achieved a lot the previous day and his research was going well. At nine o'clock, he drove up the drive of Sprite Towers and within ten minutes had begun taking notes on the portraits on the first-floor staircase.

He had already done some research into the family history before he had arrived, so when Flame had asked him if there were any Sprites who had fought in the First World War, Charles already knew the answer. He just chose not to say anything at that point, as he was curious about the reason for Flame's question. He wanted to see her reaction.

He had not believed Flame about her school project,

although it was credible. No, there was something specific she wanted to find out. He knew there was a lot more to the Sprite Sisters than met the eye. Indeed, he had been well briefed on their magic powers before he arrived.

So Charles carried on with his work. He recorded things on his digital voice recorder. He scribbled in the smart black notebook he always carried. Anybody seeing him would have thought that he was doing a legitimate piece of research on a colourful family. And he was.

But there was also another reason that Charles Smythson was standing in Sprite Towers.

He was looking for a box – a box that contained a plan. And it seemed he was not alone.

He had the sense that his young distant cousins were also urgently searching for something in the house. Something about the way they had been going up and down, and from room to room had alerted him. He did not believe that they were playing a game, as they had said.

The question was, were they looking for the same thing as he was?

Time would tell, thought Charles, as he moved up to the next family portrait, a seventeenth-century oil painting of an old woman with a black bonnet, a white lace collar and very beady eyes. She looks a real barrel of laughs, he thought, as he studied the brushwork on the painting – a portrait of Sybil Sprite.

He looked at her face and wondered if she had the magic power that ran through the Sprite family. Intuitively, he guessed that she had. There was something about her eyes – a depth, a sense of fierceness and an ability to see right through things.

He had seen that look in his young cousins. Each of them seemed to look right through him at times.

He stopped for a moment, gauging where everybody was in the house. Downstairs in the hallway, the big grandfather clock ticked. The house was still.

The girls are at the caravan, he thought. Ottalie – where is she? He heard the sound of the piano. She's giving a piano lesson in the dining room, he thought. And Colin? He's gone off to his office in town.

Charles waited a few seconds more, listening carefully. Then he walked along the first-floor corridor and opened the door to Colin and Ottalie Sprite's bedroom.

Shutting the door behind him, he moved in to the room and cast his eyes around. It was a big, airy room with a high ceiling, cream walls, pale taupe curtains and a pale mushroom-brown carpet.

He moved swiftly towards the first of two tall elegant wooden chests, glancing at the silver-framed family photographs on top. Then, quickly, he opened the drawers one by one. He looked inside each, gently feeling underneath the neatly folded clothes. No, it's not here. Right, the second chest, he thought, and made a similar search. Nothing there, either.

He moved back to the door, opened it slightly and listened. Still quiet.

Now the wardrobe, he thought, and began to search quickly and efficiently through the shelves and drawers and racks of clothes, which ran the length of one wall.

But no, it was not there.

He stood in the middle of the room. Where *is* it? I've looked in the dining room, the drawing room, the dining room and Colin's study, he thought. I'd better check the girls' rooms, the attics and the cupboards. It *must* be here somewhere . . .

What about Marilyn Sprite's sitting room and bedroom, he thought. It could be there . . . I'd better check that now, if I can.

He glanced quickly around Colin and Ottalie Sprite's bedroom to check that everything looked as it should do, then opened the door and listened. Silence.

Shutting the bedroom door quietly behind him, he moved on to the corridor. He was just about to walk towards Marilyn Sprite's rooms, when he heard the Sprite Sisters burst in through the kitchen door. Instantly, Charles climbed to the top of the first-floor staircase and studied a portrait.

'Good morning,' he said, turning to smile at the girls, as they raced up past him.

'Morning, Charles!' they replied.

'Oh Flame – I've found some portraits which may be of interest to you,' said Charles.

The eldest Sprite Sister stopped and looked around at her sisters. Then she said, 'Oh – good!'

Charles watched the girls, intently. There was a feeling of anticipation, tension almost, between them. 'Please show us,' said Flame.

Charles led them to the second-floor staircase. Amongst a number of portraits hanging there, he pointed to a large oil painting in a gilt frame. The Sprite Sisters crowded around and gazed up at the face of a young man with dark curly hair.

'As you probably know, this is your great-grandfather, Frederick Sprite – Sidney Sprite's eldest son,' said Charles.

Flame nodded. 'Grandma told us that,' she said.

'The portrait was painted in 1939, when Fred was forty-three years old. Well, he served as a captain in the army in the Great War, but thankfully survived and returned to Sprite Towers. He took over Sidney's toffee manufacturing business and lived in the house.'

'So, he is Grandad Sheldon's father,' stated Marina.

'Yes, that's right,' replied Charles. He studied the face, then turned to Marina and said, 'You've inherited his same dark, curly hair.'

Marina smiled. 'But he's got dark brown eyes – and mine are blue,' she said.

'Handsome chap though, wouldn't you agree?' asked Charles.

'Yes, he is,' replied Marina.

Charles waited for a few seconds, aware that the Sprite Sisters looked excited – as if they were holding their breath. Then he said, 'I've found another portrait that I think might be of interest to you.'

'Where it is?' asked Flame, her face bright with excitement.

'Follow me,' said Charles.

They walked up the stairs to the attics. There, propped up on the floor against the corridor wall was a huge portrait of a young man in army uniform.

'I've never seen this before – who is it?' asked Flame.

Charles gazed down at the portrait and waited for a few seconds. He could hear the Sprite Sisters breathing. Then he said, 'I found this painting at the back of a cupboard up here. This is George Sprite.'

'George Sprite?' repeated Flame.

'Yes,' said Charles, watching her face. 'Weren't you looking for someone called George?'

Flame blushed, uncomfortable under Charles's gaze.

'How do you know it's George Sprite?' asked Marina.

Charles looked around at her. 'Well, I know the Sprite family tree and who's who – and the date this portrait was painted. I've worked out that it's George Sprite, Sidney's second son – Fred's younger brother.'

'Oh,' replied Marina. She looked at her sisters, then said quickly, 'Well, he's – he's a nice-looking young man – but why does he look so sad?'

'What happened to him?' asked Flame.

'Marina's right – he probably was sad,' said Charles. 'This portrait was painted while George was on leave, home at Sprite Towers, in the spring of 1917. Shortly afterwards, he returned to the Front in Belgium.'

Charles looked at the girls as they waited. Then he said, 'He was killed a few months later at the Battle of Passchendaele – just nineteen years old.'

The Sprite Sisters were upset. 'Oh no,' they cried. 'How awful!'

Charles sighed heavily. 'Yes,' he said. 'There were so many young men like him who lost their lives in the trenches. It was a *terrible* war.'

Flame stared hard at the face of the young man. 'Poor George,' she said. Then she turned to Charles. 'Why was this portrait hidden away in a cupboard up here? It's a wonderful painting.'

Charles shook his head. 'It's a mystery to me, Flame,' he replied. 'There are letters to show that Sidney and Mim Sprite were devastated when they heard the news of George's death. He was Sidney's favourite son. I would have normally expected to see a painting like this over the top of the stairs – somewhere prominent.'

'How odd,' said Flame.

Charles continued, 'Sidney commissioned this portrait just before George left. Perhaps he knew he would not come home.'

'Maybe George knew he wouldn't, too,' added Marina, quietly. 'That's why his eyes are so sad.'

Charles nodded.

They all stared silently at the young Sprite who never came home.

Then Charles said, 'George was reputed to have been a very *special* boy.' As he said the word 'special', he turned to look at Flame's face. Would she ask more questions, he wondered, noticing that the sisters exchanged glances.

They were quiet, however, and the only sound was of their breathing.

Suddenly, out of nowhere, *Beeeep!* It was the squeaking noise that he'd heard on Wednesday morning, when the girls were standing with him on the staircase.

Charles started. Ash jumped – and stared at Charles, her

mouth open. Ash looked at Charles and Charles looked at Ash.

Flame, Marina and Ariel looked at them both, surprised.

I must get my hands on whatever is making that noise, thought Charles. There's something Ash has that I need to know about.

'Let's go down now,' said Ash suddenly, her face taut – and she ran off, down the wide mahogany staircase.

Immediately, Ariel followed her. Flame and Marina hesitated, wondering what to do. Charles looked flustered, then said, 'Well, I ought to get on now – though it has been very interesting talking to you.'

Flame regained her poise and smiled brightly. 'Thank you, Charles,' she said. 'That was really helpful.'

'Helpful?'

'For my project,' said Flame. 'I know where to start now.'

'Oh yes, your *project*,' he said, with a sudden, dazzling smile. 'Good!'

Flame and Marina followed Ariel over the lawn.

When they got back to the caravan, Ash – usually so calm and steady – sat huddled on her bunk, tears pouring down her face.

'What is it?' asked Flame, sitting down beside her.

'What's up, sis?' asked Marina, sitting down the other side of Ash and stroking her tufty chestnut hair. Ariel plopped down opposite.

'He heard it! I *know* he heard it!' said Ash.

'Was it the magic stone again?' asked Flame.

'Yes!' cried Ash.

They were silent for a moment, then Flame said, 'I noticed Charles looked at you very intently, just before you ran off.'

'He gave me the same look when it squeaked before,' said Ash. 'You know, yesterday on the stairs. The stone squeaked then and I'm certain he heard it!'

They were silent. Then Ash burst out, 'The stone will give away the secret of our magic powers! Charles will find out – and then what will happen?'

'Calm down, Ash,' said Flame, gently. 'Charles probably thinks it's your mobile phone – like Marina said yesterday.'

'There's no reason why he would know we had magic powers,' agreed Marina.

'Do you really think so?' asked Ash, worried.

'Of course,' said Flame, though she was beginning to feel less sure. How could they be certain what Charles knew about their magic powers? He was a Sprite, after all.

They were silent for a moment, each lost in their thoughts.

Then Ariel broke in. 'Let's go and have a bike race!'

'Good idea,' agreed Flame.

Ash smiled, wanly. 'Okay,' she agreed.

The girls went outside and picked up their bicycles at the side of the camp.

For the next half hour they tore around, laughing and swerving.

Somewhere in Flame's mind, however, an alarm bell was ringing.

Upstairs, Charles looked out of Marilyn Sprite's bedroom window and saw the girls cycling around the big lawn. As soon as he thought he was safe, he had come here directly.

He moved quickly around the sitting room. He pulled open the drawers on the rosewood desk, one by one. When he had searched every drawer and cupboard in the sitting room, he moved through to the bedroom.

Charles looked everywhere, and was so engrossed that he did not hear Marilyn Sprite come into her room until she was standing right behind him. He was peering down into the drawer at the bottom of her wardrobe, when he heard a very fierce voice shout: '*What on earth do you think you are you doing?*'

Charles Smythson leaped up and spun around in astonishment. There in front of him was a tall woman with a strawberry-blond bob and fierce green eyes! In her right hand she held a small suitcase.

He gasped. Marilyn Sprite! She was supposed to be away – not home until tomorrow. His mind raced as she looked at him with a face like thunder.

She started to shout again, '*WHAT DO YOU—*' when Charles drew a sharp breath and stared into her eyes with an icy glare.

Before another word came out of her mouth, Marilyn Sprite stood completely still. It was as if she'd been frozen. One minute she moved, the next instant she was fixed in time and space – her mouth open, her eyes wide, glazed.

Charles gasped, his heart pounding. Oh my God, he thought, staring at the frozen woman in front of him. Then, very quickly, he lifted his right arm and put his hand in front of Marilyn's face. Drawing his fingers together, his pulled back his hand – as if dragging something out of her mind. With a flick of his wrist, he threw it down towards the floor.

In that instant, Charles Smythson used his magic power to remove the memory in Marilyn Sprite's mind that led up to that moment.

Then he walked out of the room.

When Marilyn came to a minute later, Charles Smythson had disappeared, back to his research on the second floor of the house. He was now standing there, looking at one of the portraits and making notes in his black notebook. But anyone looking closely at him in that moment would have seen he was shaking with shock.

I wonder if Ottalie heard Marilyn shout, he thought. I wonder if anyone saw her come up the stairs . . . Oh my God – what have I done?

Marilyn Sprite stood in her room and wondered what she was doing.

Now, what did I come up here for, she wondered. She had forgotten. She looked down at her case.

I must have come up here to put this away, she decided. She put the case on a chair and looked around her room.

Not one bit of the memory of her confrontation with Charles Smythson remained in her mind. She did not recall that she had found him searching in her wardrobe.

She did not remember how he had stared into her eyes and used his dark magic to disempower her.

Up on the staircase, Charles looked down and watched

Marilyn Sprite descend to the hallway.

That was close, he thought to himself. That was very close. And he leaned against the wall.

A few minutes later, he heard the the Sprite Sisters chattering with delight at their grandmother's early return to Sprite Towers.

He heard Ottalie say, 'I'm glad you're home, Marilyn – there's so much to do for the fête on Saturday.'

'Yes, it's lucky Valerie returned early,' replied Grandma.

I hope my magic has worked, he thought, anxiously. I won't know for sure until I go down and meet Marilyn Sprite. If she does not recognise me, then I'm safe . . .

Half an hour later, when Ottalie called him down to lunch, he walked into the kitchen.

'Charles – meet my mother-in-law, Marilyn Sprite,' said Ottalie.

He smiled, held out his hand and moved towards the tall, elegant woman with the dancer's stance. She smiled back – and put out her hand.

'So you're Charles,' she said, shaking his hand.

'Yes, it's good to meet you, Marilyn,' he replied.

All through lunch, he waited for a flicker of recognition in her eyes – but there was none.

My magic is getting more powerful, he thought.

That evening at the camp, Flame built up the campfire. Marina boiled a pan of milk and made mugs of thick hot chocolate. Ash cut four large slices of Mum's homemade fruitcake and Ariel handed them out on plastic plates. Then the Sprite Sisters sat down on their stools around the fire.

'Well, we know who George Sprite is now,' said Flame, staring at the fire.

'Yes, but we still haven't found the box – and we've looked everywhere,' said Ariel, sipping her hot chocolate.

'And we still don't know what the secret of the towers is,' said Marina.

'And Charles *may* know I have a magic stone,' said Ash. 'I feel him watching me all the time.'

Her words hung in the air. Flame drew breath. The niggling worry in the back of her mind came forward again.

That is true, she thought. Charles may know about the stone – and it does feel as if he's watching us very closely. If knows we have a magic *stone*, he may wonder if we have magic *powers* . . .

'We must be very careful to keep everything secret,' said Flame, looking around at her sisters. 'We must not give away anything – and Ariel, you must not say a thing about Sidney or let anyone see you talking to him. Do you understand?'

'Yes,' replied Ariel, chewing a large mouthful of fruitcake.

'I managed to get a few minutes with Grandma this afternoon, without Mum about,' said Flame. 'I showed her George Sprite's letter – and she said we should be very careful.'

'Did she know about George Sprite?' asked Marina.

'Only a little,' replied Flame.

'Did you tell her about the squeaking stone?' asked Ash.

'Yes,' nodded Flame.

'Did she know about the magic box?' asked Marina.

'No, she'd never heard about that,' said Flame.

'Did she have any ideas about where we might find it?' asked Ash.

'No – not really,' replied Flame.

'What did Grandma say we should do?' asked Marina.

'She said we must keep the letter well hidden,' said Flame.

'I've put it under my mattress, but what shall I do about the magic stone?' asked Ash. 'Wouldn't it be better to leave it in the caravan, in case it squeaks again in front of Charles?'

Ash waited for an answer as Flame stared at the fire, intently.

What was it, this feeling of unease, thought Flame. I feel as if something is closing in around us. The stone would be out of earshot if we left it here – but would it be safe?

As her mind focused, she had the sudden sense that they should keep both the stone and the letter close. She turned to Ash and said, 'I think you should keep hold of the stone, Ash – and that I should keep the letter in my pocket when we leave the camp.'

'But what if the stone squeaks again?' said Ash.

'I still think you should keep it close,' said Flame. 'If it squeaks, it's because it's telling you something.'

Overhead, dark swirling clouds crossed the evening sky. Wind rustled through tall pine trees. The Sprite Sisters shivered.

'It suddenly feels quite chilly,' said Marina. 'I'm going to get my jumper. Do you want yours, too?'

Yes, they did, they agreed. They all felt chilly.

Flame stared again at the fire. As the flames licked around the burning wood, she had the sense, somewhere deep in her mind, that something had changed. She could not see it – but she could feel it.

I won't say anything, she thought. I won't say anything until I know what this is – but something is not right.

As Marina handed her sisters their jumpers, she felt their mood sinking. 'Why don't we sing for a bit?' she suggested.

'Goodie!' said Ariel.

'We could get our instruments,' suggested Ash.

'No, we'll have to go inside and disturb the grown-ups,' said Marina.

'And we can't leave the instruments out here in the damp,' said Flame.

Marina sat down on her stool and started to sing a folk song. Her voice rang loud and clear through the night air and their spirits lifted. Flame, Ash and Ariel clapped their hands and sang the choruses and the harmonies.

Then Ash reached for a large saucepan, turned it over and started to drum on the bottom with her hands, as if she was playing a tabla.

Flame found two short, hard sticks and banged them together. They made a satisfying clacking sound. Then she grabbed two spoons, which went 'clunk' when she banged them together.

Ariel jumped up and said, 'I've got my harmonica in the caravan!' and rushed to get it.

Suddenly, they had rhythm – they had music. Marina sang out a second folk song, which got faster and faster and the girls played louder and louder.

In the kitchen of Sprite Towers, Mum, Dad, Grandma and

Charles were sitting at the table drinking coffee. On the floor in front of the Aga, Bert sat up and lifted his ears.

Mum looked up and listened. 'What's that noise?' she said.

They stopped talking. Dad stood up, went to the door and opened it. 'It's the girls!' he said, smiling. 'They're singing!'

Bert ran outside and lolloped over the lawn towards the camp.

Mum, Grandma and Charles moved to the doorway and followed Dad outside on to the terrace. They stood there, listening.

'It sounds wonderful!' said Mum, clapping her hands together.

'Yes, they're having fun,' agreed Dad, putting his arm around her.

Grandma smiled. 'The caravan was a good idea, Colin!'

Charles Smythson stood beside them. Outwardly, he looked happy and relaxed. Inwardly, his stomach churned – as if a large knot was tightening. As he stood in the darkness listening to the Sprite Sisters' singing, he thought how lovely this family were.

I don't want to hurt the Sprites, I really don't, he thought. But I have a task to fulfil – and I *have* to fulfil it.

Mum interrupted his thoughts. 'Shall we go down to the camp?' she asked, looking around. 'It would be lovely to join in with the singing!'

'No, love, let's leave the girls this evening,' said Dad. 'We'll go down another time. Shame to disturb them when they're having such fun.'

'Yes – another time,' agreed Mum, wiping a tear away from her eye. 'It reminds me of my own childhood. We're so lucky to have all this.'

'Yes, we are,' said Dad, hugging her.

As the flames on the campfire started to lessen and the air grew chillier, the Sprite Sisters climbed into their sleeping bags and went to sleep.

Deep in the night, as the waning moon shone down on the old white caravan, Flame had a dream.

She was standing in the West Tower. In front of her, in the middle of the room, appeared a door. She reached to open it, walked forward and looked through the doorway.

Then she saw it: a great swoosh of coloured light that stretched up in front of her and seemed to pass through the wall of the tower.

CHAPTER SIX

THE MISSING STONE

'I HAD a really strange dream,' said Flame, as they woke on Friday morning in the caravan.

'What was it about?' asked Ash, rubbing her eyes.

'We were in the West Tower – and there was this light,' said Flame.

'What sort of light?' asked Marina, sitting up.

'Like a big rainbow – only it wasn't a rainbow,' said Flame. 'It was a huge band of coloured light that came out of the floor, and went up and out through the wall of the tower.'

'Which way did it go out of the tower – east, south, north or west?' asked Ash.

'Oh, heck,' replied Flame. She thought for a moment, then said, 'I think it pointed east – out towards the East Tower.'

'I've never seen anything like that in the tower,' said Ariel, blearily. She pushed back her soft blond hair from her face.

Flame laughed. 'Neither have I! It was a dream!'

'I wonder what it means?' asked Marina. 'Do you think it has anything to do with the magic box? You know how your dreams sometimes have warnings for you, Flame?'

'True,' said Flame. She'd had a horrible nightmare only a few weeks before, which warned her that Glenda Glass would try to hurt them at the school concert.

Flame took note of her dreams. But what did this one mean? A band of light that went out through the tower wall: what was that about?

There was a shout from outside. 'Come on, Ash – we've got to check the vegetables!' It was Dad, standing by the camp boundary.

Today was the last day before the Village Fête – an important day for Ash and her father, who would be submitting their prize vegetables and flowers to the Annual Horticultural Competition. That morning they had to select the things they would pick the following morning.

'He's up early,' said Marina.

'Well, it's important,' said Ash, pulling on her jeans and T-shirt. She opened the door of the caravan and shouted, 'Just coming, Dad!'

'Okay, I'll get started.' And he walked off with his long-legged stride towards the vegetable garden.

While Flame, Marina and Ariel cooked eggy bread on the campfire and ate their breakfast, Ash and Dad peered at the runner bean plants. These grew on three sets of canes, each pinned in the ground like tall, pointed witches' hats. The bean plants grew round and round the canes and had big green leaves and pretty red flowers. Ash and Dad looked at the clumps of hanging beans, searching for three beans that had a perfect shape and were exactly the same size.

'What about these ones?' said Ash, pointing.

Dad bent his long legs and peered down. 'Yes, they look good,' he said. 'Let's hope they're the same size tomorrow when we pick them. Now what about the courgettes?'

They moved to the courgette bed and for the next few minutes clambered about looking for three perfect courgettes, identical in size and colour.

'Should we give them some water?' said Ash.

'Good idea – just a tad,' agreed Dad, and he got up to get the hose. 'We'll dig the carrots tomorrow morning.'

'Do you think we stand a good chance, Dad?' asked Ash, kneeling in the courgette bed.

'Absolutely!' said Dad. 'Sprite Towers vegetables are second to none!'

'Are we good gardeners?'

'Top notch!'

Dad looked up. The air was August-muggy, but huge clouds swooshed across the sky. One minute, the garden was bright and sunny, the next it was dark with black clouds threatening rain.

'Feels like we could be building up to a storm,' he said. 'Let's just hope the rain holds off until after the fête tomorrow.'

Ash gazed up at the sky. The humid air gave her the sudden feeling that something was closing in on her – and she shuddered, slightly.

What is it, she wondered, as she got up to help Dad with the watering.

By the time Ash got back to the camp, her sisters had finished breakfast. Marina and Ariel had gone off to see to the rabbits and guinea pigs. Every morning in the summer, they moved the animals' hutches a little way over the lawn, so they always had a fresh supply of grass.

'You okay?' said Flame, noticing a look of tension in Ash's face.

Ash nodded and the feeling passed. Now she was hungry.

'Would you like some eggy bread?' said Flame. 'I left two bits for you. I'll cook it for you, if you like.'

'Yum – yes, please,' said Ash, sitting down on a stool beside the campfire. 'The vegetables are looking good. Dad reckons we should win some of the competitions. I love being in the garden growing things – especially with him. It's so peaceful.'

'Yes, I know you do.' Flame smiled. 'There's some orange juice over there.' She pointed to a carton on the grass.

Ash grabbed a knife and fork, a mug and some juice, then sat down by the fire and watched her sister.

'Where's George's letter?' asked Flame, lifting the eggy bread into the sizzling frying pan.

'It's still under my mattress,' replied Ash.

'Good,' said Flame. 'And what about your stone?'

'It's in my pocket,' said Ash, touching it. 'Why?'

'Just checking,' replied Flame. 'If you pop and get the letter, I'll stick it in my pocket. I'd feel happier keeping it with us.'

'Okay,' said Ash and went back into the caravan. A minute later, Ash handed Flame the letter and Flame handed Ash a plate of eggy bread and a bottle of tomato sauce.

'Thanks,' said Ash and tucked in.

As she ate, Flame sat down on a stool. 'Thanks for getting this,' she said and looked in the envelope. There was George's letter and tucked in the bottom corner was the little metal key. All okay, nothing missing, she thought. She closed the envelope and put it into her right jeans pocket.

'Mum's taking us swimming this afternoon,' said Ash.

Flame smiled. 'Yeah, I know. That'll be fun.' She stared at the campfire. 'I wonder where this box is . . . I wish we could find it.'

'Hmm,' agreed Ash, munching.

'It doesn't feel as if we are any closer,' said Flame.

Charles Smythson was itching to go to the camp and hunt around for the box while the girls were out that afternoon, but Dad was working in his office at the back of the house and Grandma was weeding the rose garden. It would be impossible to go to the camp without passing her. So Charles paced anxiously along the corridor, staring at the portraits.

I must find the box and I must get hold of the thing that keeps squeaking in Ash's pocket, he thought.

Although she had no memory of seeing Charles in her room,

Grandma had been watching him like a hawk since Flame had told her that he seemed to have heard Ash's stone squeak. He might be charming, but he was a Sprite and Glenda Glass's nephew – and he might have heard the stone. Could it mean he had the magic power that ran through the family? What if he knew that her granddaughters were in possession of a hundred-year-old letter that described a magic box? What then? They could be in danger . . .

Luck was on Charles's side later that afternoon. The Sprite Sisters were ravenous when they came back from swimming and sat around the kitchen table eating large pieces of Grandma's special chocolate cake. Mum poured glasses of elderflower cordial.

Then Ash said, 'I'll just go up and get a jumper.' As she ran out of the kitchen and up the wide mahogany staircase, Charles was standing on the second-floor corridor, looking at some small watercolour paintings. Ash rounded the corner and virtually bumped into him. Her sudden appearance surprised them both – he saw her gasp with shock.

Charles acted instantly. All he needed was for Ash to look at him. That would be enough to use his magic power.

'Ash!' he said, with his dazzling smile. 'Did you have a good swim?'

'Er, yes, thank you,' she replied, looking up at him, politely. An instant later, she stood as if frozen on the corridor. Her eyes were glazed and she stared ahead, blankly.

'Ash, give me the thing that makes the squeaking noise,' said Charles.

Ash reached into her jeans pocket and drew out the stone.

'Give it to me,' repeated Charles.

Ash handed him the stone.

At the same time, Charles moved his hand in front of her face, as he had done with Grandma, and drew out the memory from her mind and threw it away.

Then, whilst Ash remained motionless, he walked quickly down the stairs to the first floor corridor and stood, out of view, around the corner.

When Ash came to and walked down the stairs a minute later, Charles was out of sight.

Out of sight, out of mind, he thought.

Ash returned to the kitchen, empty-handed.

'I thought you went up to get your jumper,' said Mum.

'Did I?' said Ash.

Mum made a face at Ash, as if to say, 'Wake up!'

Ariel giggled. 'If you're not careful, you'll soon be as forgetful as me!' she said.

After the girls left the table, Mum went upstairs. Grandma sat there a while longer, sipping her cup of tea. Somewhere, far back in her mind, she had the resonance of something to do with something she had gone upstairs for. Had she, too, gone up to find a jumper and come down empty-handed? What was it, she wondered. She could not remember.

Her thoughts turned to Charles Smythson. The memory of Glenda's recent attack on Sprite Towers was still too sharp in her mind for Marilyn Sprite to be anything less than wary with a stranger in the house.

And Charles *is* a stranger, she thought. Really we know very little about him. Even if he barely knows Glenda, he's still her nephew.

As she thought of Glenda Glass, Marilyn Sprite's jaw tightened and her body tensed. She remembered how she lost her own magic power, defending herself forty-five years ago against Glenda's attack.

Glenda Glass, the woman who tried to get us out of Sprite Towers, she thought. Glenda Glass, the woman who stole my inheritance . . .

Then her thoughts moved to her granddaughters, George's letter and the hunt for the magic box. They must keep this safe, she thought. Charles Smythson is wandering around the house – and I must be watchful.

The Sprite Sisters ran down to the camp.

As Ash stood by the campfire, she instinctively reached for the stone in her pocket.

'*The stone!*' she cried out, standing by the caravan. '*Where's my stone?*'

Flame, Marina and Ariel ran up to her.

'*Where's the stone?*' Ash's face was white and she was spinning around looking on the ground.

'Are you sure you haven't got it?' asked Flame.

'It was in my jeans pocket!' cried Ash, now in tears.

'When did you last feel it there?' asked Marina.

'I don't know.' Ash stopped and rubbed her forehead.

'Did you have it after swimming?' asked Ariel.

Ash stared ahead, trying to think. 'Yes, no – I'm not sure.'

'What about when we had tea in the kitchen?' asked Flame.

Ash stared at the grass. Her head felt all fuzzy when she thought about the stone. 'I don't know,' she said.

'We'll find it,' said Flame. 'It could have fallen out of your pocket in the car, or when we were at the table.'

'It's never fallen out of my pocket before,' said Ash. 'I'm very careful with it.'

'Yes, we know you are,' said Flame, reassuringly.

'Perhaps it fell out while you were changing at the pool,' suggested Ariel.

'No, I folded up my jeans really carefully,' cried Ash. 'Oh, we'll never find it!'

'Let's look on the lawn and make our way back to the house,' suggested Flame.

The four Sprite Sisters walked side by side, back up to the house, all the time scanning the grass. Then they went into the kitchen. Grandma was standing in front of the Aga, making jam for the fête. She looked around as they burst in. 'What's happened?' she asked, seeing Ash's white face.

'Ash has lost her magic stone,' said Flame.

'Oh dear!' said Grandma. 'You'll find it, love. Just retrace your steps carefully.'

'Where are Mum and Dad and Charles?' asked Flame.

'They're in the drawing room,' replied Grandma. 'Charles is telling them about his research. I should just leave them be for now.'

Flame looked at Ash. 'Did you go into the drawing room this afternoon?'

Ash shook her head. 'I don't think so.'

'Okay, we can rule that out, but it may be here in the kitchen – and didn't you go upstairs to get a jumper, while we were having tea?' said Flame.

'I don't remember,' replied Ash.

'It's not like you to forget things,' commented Marina.

'No,' agreed Ash, quietly.

For the next ten minutes, the Sprite Sisters searched the kitchen floor and hall, then walked up the stairs to Ash's room.

Nothing.

'It's not here,' said Ash, miserably.

'Let's look in Mum's car,' suggested Marina.

But the stone wasn't there, either.

'Okay, let's go back down to the caravan,' said Flame. 'We can check the lawn again as we go.'

And back they went.

'Flame, you have still got George's letter, haven't you?' asked Ash anxiously, as she opened the caravan door.

'Yes, it's right here,' said Flame, patting her jeans pocket.

The four girls stood in the old white caravan. They opened cupboard doors and looked under the four mattresses. Then they went outside and looked around the camp. They looked everywhere. Still nothing.

'So where is it?' asked Ash, her face pale.

'Perhaps it will squeak and you'll hear it and find it,' said Marina.

Ash smiled a sad smile.

A minute later, Grandma rang the ship's bell outside the kitchen door, to summon them to supper. The Sprite Sisters ran back over the lawn and burst into the kitchen. Mum was dressing a large green salad. Dad was laying the table and Charles was pouring out glasses of water. Grandma was spooning a creamy sauce over pieces of baked fish in a large, colourful dish.

'Go and wash your hands,' said Mum, as the Sprite Sisters tumbled past.

'Evening, girls,' smiled Charles.

They smiled as they dashed through to the cloakroom in the hallway. Flame, Marina and Ash were soon back in the kitchen.

'Where's Ariel?' asked Dad.

'I dunno – she was with us washing her hands,' said Marina.

The family and Charles sat down at the table. Grandma served out the fish on to plates and Mum added servings of new potatoes.

Ariel walked in and quietly took her place.

'Ah, there you are,' said Dad. 'Wondered where you'd got to.'

Ariel smiled at Dad.

Oh no, thought Flame, she's got that 'look'.

Flame and Marina exchanged glances. They knew their little sister was up to something.

The family talked and started to eat. Ariel took her plate and helped herself to salad.

Mum, Dad and Charles talked about the portraits. Grandma and the Sprite Sisters listened.

Then, as everybody was relaxed and just as Charles was lifting the salad bowl to take another helping, Ariel looked at him with a completely straight face – in the way that only Ariel could – and said, 'Charles, please would you give Ash her stone. I think you have it in your right pocket.'

Charles held the salad bowl, suspended in mid-air – then he laughed. He laid the bowl down on the table, aware of the eyes of the entire family suddenly on him. He smiled, disarmingly, as his mind raced to think of a way out. For a split second he stared at Ariel and she stared back at him, her grey eyes wide and expectant.

Dad broke in, 'What's this, Ariel? What stone?' He looked at Charles for clarification.

'Ash has a special stone she carries about – and she lost it this afternoon,' said Ariel. 'I think Charles has it.'

'Do you, Charles?' asked Dad.

In a flash, Charles smiled his dazzling smile, put his right hand into his pocket, drew out the stone and held it out on the palm of his hand. 'Abracadabra! Is this the stone?' he asked. 'I found it this afternoon.'

Ash jumped up and pushed back her chair. 'Yes!' she said, reaching out. 'Please can I have it!'

'Of course!' Charles leaned over and handed it to her.

Ash's face lit up with a look of absolute relief.

While Mum and Dad watched her, Grandma, Flame, Marina and Ariel were looking at Charles. He smiled around at them, sensing their gaze.

Have they sussed me, he wondered, as he took a sip of water. That was too close, he thought, feeling sweat break out in beads on his brow – a fact not missed by Grandma's keen eyes, nor Flame's.

He's lying, they both thought together and exchanged glances. But how did he take it?

Ash cradled her magic stone in her hands, then smiled at her sisters. She was so relieved to have it back.

Ash turned to Charles. 'Where did you find it?'

'I picked it up from the driveway just outside the front door,' he replied. 'I thought it had some interesting markings.'

Flame was wondering if Charles had intended to tell them about the stone, when Dad said, 'Can I have a look, Ash?'

He took the magic stone from her and held it up. 'Hmm, what a lovely stone,' he said, turning it over. 'Interesting markings. That crossed circle motif is all over the house.'

'Yes, I noticed that, Colin,' said Charles. 'The crossed circle is carved on the fireplaces; it's in the plaster coving in a number of the rooms. And it's also in the towers.'

Flame looked at her sisters and they at her. We must look more closely, thought Flame.

Then Mum asked to see at the stone and agreed it had unusual markings. 'You've never shown us this before, Ash,' she said. 'It's beautiful. Where did you find it?'

'In one of the cupboards,' replied Ash.

'Funny thing to find in a cupboard,' said Mum. 'Mind you, you never know what you will find in the cupboards of Sprite Towers!'

Charles lifted his glass of wine and gazed at Ariel. 'How did you know I had the stone in my pocket?'

Ariel looked at him with her wide grey eyes and said, 'Sidney Sprite told me you had it.'

Mum swallowed hard and Dad guffawed.

Charles smiled. 'Really? How interesting! Sidney Sprite, eh?'

'Well, he was right,' said Ariel. 'You did have the stone in your pocket.'

'True,' acknowledged Charles, making a mental note never again to underestimate the youngest Sprite Sister, despite her dreamy demeanour.

'Please excuse my funny little daughter, Charles!' said Dad, with a big grin on his face. 'She has a very vivid imagination!'

Ariel shrugged, then glanced at Grandma, who smiled at her little granddaughter – a look that was not lost on Charles.

For the rest of the meal, Grandma watched the handsome young man with the dazzling smile even more closely. He felt the strength of her piercing green eyes and only calmed down by assuring himself that Marilyn Sprite, despite her suspicions, still had no knowledge of his magic power.

When the Sprite Sisters had left to go back to their camp, Dad made coffee and Mum, Charles and Grandma went through to the conservatory. Mum lit a lamp and some candles and they sat down in the large wicker chairs.

'It's very elegant room, Ottalie,' commented Charles.

'It was built with the house in 1910,' she replied. 'It's a useful room to have on cooler evenings. The summer seems to be passing very quickly. Another few weeks and the girls will be back at school.'

Charles smiled. 'They're lovely girls,' he said. Then he added, 'And unusual.'

Mum took this in good jest, 'Yes,' she agreed. 'They certainly are that.'

They were silent for a moment, then Grandma asked quietly, 'Where's Glenda Glass gone on holiday, Charles?'

She knew from his expression that she had taken him off guard, but he answered casually. 'I think Stephen said she'd gone to the south of France. She has a house there.'

'Oh,' said Grandma and shot a look at Mum. Ottalie and Colin Sprite might not know about their daughters' magic powers, nor Glenda's, but Marilyn had told them of her suspicions that Glenda had stolen her inheritance – money which had gone missing in the south of France.

'The south of France, eh,' said Mum. For an instant she felt uncomfortable. There was something wolfish in Charles's smile, she realised. All those big white teeth, perhaps.

They were silent for a moment, then Grandma asked, 'How well do you know Glenda?'

'I have hardly ever spoken to her,' replied Charles, quickly.

'That surprises me,' said Grandma.

'Why?'

Grandma was saved answering by Dad, who came in with a large tray of coffee and cups. 'Here we go!' he said.

As he poured the coffee, Charles asked him about his new architectural project and the subject of Glenda receded.

The weather was changing. Huge clouds billowed through the sky and the wind began to blow. Every few minutes, the old white caravan was in complete darkness, as the clouds covered the sliver of waning moon.

The Sprite Sisters lay in their sleeping bags on their bunks, the torch propped up in the middle. Their faces glowed eerily in the light; everything else in the caravan was pitch black.

'Charles looked *so* surprised when you asked him for the stone!' laughed Marina.

'Yes,' giggled Ariel.

'I told you he'd heard it,' said Ash. 'I think he took it deliberately.'

'What – you mean, took it from you?' asked Flame. 'How would he do that without you knowing?'

'I don't know,' said Ash, thoughtfully. 'I just don't remember losing it.'

Flame turned to Ariel. 'Did you ask Sidney how Charles got hold of the stone?'

'Yes,' said Ariel, propped up on her elbow.

'Well, what did he say?'

'He said we'd have to figure it out for ourselves, that he wouldn't tell us everything.'

'That sounds like Mrs Duggery – she said things like that to us,' said Marina.

'Sidney did say that we had to look more closely at things,' said Ariel.

'Look more closely at things . . . ' Flame repeated. 'I wonder what he means.'

They were silent.

'It sort of suggests something could be right under our noses and we're not seeing it,' continued Flame.

'Or feeling it,' added Marina, who was more likely to feel things rather than see them.

'True,' agreed Flame.

Then Ariel said, 'Do you think Charles Smythson has magic powers?'

Flame, Marina and Ash sat up. 'Why do you ask that?' they chorused.

'There's something about his eyes,' said Ariel. 'I noticed it at the table – his eyes have magic in them.'

Flame, Marina and Ash thought about this. They had found that their little sister had incredible insight at times. It was part of her power of Air.

'You think he may have power in his eyes?' asked Marina. 'That's amazing!'

'He's a Sprite, don't forget – it's possible,' said Ash.

'And he's on the side of the family that the bad magic runs through,' added Flame.

'How would he use power in his eyes?' asked Marina.

'Perhaps he can make you do things,' suggested Ariel.

Flame sat up even straighter. 'Oh my goodness – I think I know how he got the stone!'

'How?' her sisters asked.

'Ash, when you went up to get your jumper, did you meet Charles?' asked Flame. 'Was he upstairs?'

Marina, Flame and Ariel gazed at their sister through the dim light. Outside, the wind blew around the caravan.

Ash was silent. She looked baffled and shook her head. 'It's funny – I just can't remember,' she said.

'You came down without your jumper, do you remember that?' asked Flame.

'I remember you *saying* that,' said Ash, hugging her knees.

'I bet he took the stone off you when you went upstairs – and he's somehow erased the memory of it!' said Flame, excited at her deduction.

They thought about this for a while, then Ash said, 'So where does that leave us?'

'It means,' said Flame, staring down to the floor as if she was searching for an idea. 'It means . . . it means that Charles may be here, at Sprite Towers, for some other reason.'

'And the research is a cover,' suggested Marina. 'Yeah, I see what you mean.'

'That would fit with Sidney saying that the answer was right under our noses and we weren't seeing it,' said Ariel, yawning.

'So he did take the stone off me,' said Ash.

'Yes,' said Flame. 'And that means he may try to do so again.'

'So how should we protect ourselves?' asked Ash.

Ariel lay down and yawned again. 'Don't look him in the eyes,' she said and fell asleep.

Ash and Marina settled down and within a minute were asleep too.

Flame turned off the torch, then lay on her back, her arms tucked under her head. She stared up into the dark. Outside, the tall pine trees moved in the wind and an owl screeched.

What is it that Charles is really looking for, thought Flame. And why?

What does he know that we don't know, she wondered, as she drifted off to sleep.

A few miles away at The Oaks, Charles Smythson sat in the drawing room cradling the phone in his left hand. In the other, he held a large glass of whisky. He needed to brace himself. This phone call is not going to be easy, he thought.

He was furious that the girls had got back their stone before he'd really had a chance to study it.

Why did it squeak when I was close by, twice, he wondered. I've probably given the game away, he thought, gloomily. Ash knows I heard it – and she'll have told her sisters. If I take much longer, Marilyn and the girls may deduce the truth about me.

Charles took another slug of whisky, then put down the glass on the table beside him. He passed the phone to his right hand.

What do I say, he thought. I've had no specific results other than finding – and losing – a stone that emitted squeaking noises. I've still not found this blasted box . . . I know what the reaction will be. Fury. Cold fury – and threats, more threats . . .

Damn and blast, he thought, banging his left hand down on his knee. I don't want this to mess up my research . . . It's getting late . . . I must phone now. They're an hour ahead over there.

He took a deep breath, then punched in the numbers on the handset.

Exhaling slowly, he listened to the soft beep of the dialling tone. At the other end, a voice answered.

'Glenda, hello – it's Charles.'

CHAPTER SEVEN

✴

THE VILLAGE FÊTE

✴
✴
✴

THERE WAS much excitement on Saturday morning. Dad and Ash dashed off down the garden, to pick their vegetables. With great care, they laid out in a wide box the bunch of tiny carrots, the three green runner beans, the three perfectly matching courgettes, five perfectly matching pods of green peas, three perfectly matching broad beans, six perfectly matching red tomatoes, two orange pumpkins and a green marrow. Then they picked a bunch of fragrant and colourful sweet peas and a colourful bunch of dahlias.

'I read somewhere that dahlias are the "new" sweet peas,' commented Dad.

'I still don't like them very much,' said Ash. 'They have a horrible smell and they're full of earwigs.'

'Hmm, you're right,' said Dad, holding the dahlias upside down and shaking them. Several earwigs plopped on to the ground and scuttled off.

Dad placed the bunch of flowers on the box of flowers and vegetables.

'Look at all this!' he said, proudly. 'Splendid work, Ash!'

Meanwhile, in the kitchen, Grandma, Flame and Marina baked and iced cakes for the cake stall. Ariel iced the fairy cakes and sprinkled silver fairy dust over the top.

All the proceeds from the fête would go towards the church funds. The Sprites had an ancient and beautiful church in their village and they were happy to support it.

As Mum was one of the organisers of the fête, she left early. With her car full of books for the bookstall and three jars of Grandma's strawberry jam for the jam competition, she drove to the village green where the fête would be held. On one side of the green was the village hall, where Mum had stored the boxes of junk last Monday for the bric-a-brac stall. On the other side stood the flint church with its high tower.

Mum unloaded her car and put out the books on the bookstall. Then she took Grandma's jam to the produce tent to be judged, before going into the village hall. One by one, she carried out the boxes of junk and laid out the items on the bric-a-brac stall. One of the things that she placed on the stall was the small wooden box, about the size of an old cigar box, with a crossed circle on its top.

By midday the village green was bursting with life. Everywhere people were setting up stalls and games.

Coloured ribbons and strings of flags fluttered in the wind.

'Hello, Ottalie!' people kept saying.

'Let's hope the weather holds!' she called back.

Overhead, big clouds whooshed through the sky, some bright white, some dark and threatening.

'Do you think we should cover these in case it rains, Ottalie?' said Batty Blenkinsop, who was running the book stall.

Mum looked up at the sky. 'Hmm,' she said. 'Good idea, though I think we'll make it.'

Soon, Dad and Ash were there. They laid out their vegetables in the horticultural tent, along with the other gardeners from the village.

As soon as Mum finished setting up the bric-a-brac stall, she helped out on the other stalls.

Then, seeing Dad, she called, 'Colin, let's get home and have some lunch. We need to be back by one-thirty – it opens at two.'

'Okay!' he called back.

Back they drove to Sprite Towers. After a lunch of soup, bread and cheese, Grandma and the girls carried the freshly made cakes to Mum's big red car and they all piled in.

'I'll be there in a minute,' said Dad.

'Where's Charles?' asked Mum, as she was about to climb into her car.

'Haven't seen him yet,' replied Dad.

Mum zoomed off down the drive. Dad was just locking up when Charles Smythson arrived.

'I'm just off to the fête,' said Dad. 'The others have all gone. Are you coming down?'

'I just need to check something on one of the drawing room portraits, first – but I'll be there in a short while,' said Charles.

'Okay – put the lock down on the front door when you leave, please,' said Dad. 'And make sure Bert is in the house.'

'Will do,' agreed Charles. 'See you shortly.'

Dad jumped in his old racing green-coloured sports car and bombed off down the drive.

'Perfect,' thought Charles. 'I have Sprite Towers to myself.'

Charles Smythson's fingers were almost twitching as he walked, as fast as he could, to the old white caravan.

He pulled down the handle. Ah, good, he thought. The door's not locked. He pushed it open and looked in, then climbed up the step. Now where's this blasted box, he thought.

It was tidy – Flame's influence. One by one, he opened the cupboards and pulled out clothes and blankets. He was careful to put them back neatly.

Not there, he thought. What about under the beds? One by one, he lifted up the mattresses and felt underneath.

When he got to Ash's bed – he recognised her sweater lying there – he stopped. It's not here, he thought, as he felt under the mattress – but I can *feel* it. I can *feel* something . . .

I know Ash will have the stone with her, he thought.

'Damn and blast!' said Charles, and walked out to the campfire. He could feel his heart pounding, his stress level rising.

I've *got* to find it, he thought, clenching his fists. Quickly, he looked through the boxes of food and utensils – but there was nothing there.

Then he hurried back to the house. He made his way to Dad's office and began to look through his things. He checked the things on Dad's desk, then rifled through the drawers and cupboards and searched along the shelves.

But still Charles could not find what he was looking for.

He looked at his watch. Nearly two-thirty – I must get going, he thought or they'll wonder where I am.

Charles began to feel he might explode.

Nothing. I can't believe it, he thought. I've looked *everywhere*! I've been through every room in this blasted house in the last four days.

He took care to leave everything as he had found it, then walked out of the room. In the hallway he stood, thinking. Where is it? he thought. *Where is it?*

Then, checking that Bert was inside, he pulled the front door, turned and walked to his car.

The fête was in full swing. The local Silver Band played and the sun shone. Everyone looked happy. Flame, Marina, Ash and Ariel were having a wonderful time. They threw quoits, hurled balls at the coconut shy, played hook-a-duck, spun the arrow and chanced the lucky dip. They walked around, holding their prizes and talking to their friends and neighbours.

Dad and Ash were delighted when they won a raft of prizes for their vegetables and the overall prize for 'Vegetable Grower of the Year'.

'Congratulations, Colin – you've done it again,' said Betty Carruthers, the head judge, shaking Dad's hand. She leaned over to give a small silver cup to Ash and shake her hand, too.

'Thank you,' said Ash, beaming.

On the bric-a-brac stall, Mum had a constant stream of browsers and buyers. On the cake stall, people almost fought for Marilyn Sprite's cakes. She was delighted that her strawberry jam had won first prize on the produce competition.

Standing in the middle of the fête, Flame looked around. 'I can't see Charles anywhere,' she said, but her sisters weren't listening.

I wonder where he is, she thought. A sense of uneasiness passed over her. She felt inside her pocket. George Sprite's letter was still there – and the little key. She could feel it in there, too. Thank goodness they're safe, she thought. Funny that I felt I should bring them here, just at the last minute.

Ash broke into her thoughts. 'Let's go and have a look at Mum's bric-a-brac stall,' she said.

'I want an ice cream,' said Ariel. 'I'll join you over there.'

The three older Sprite Sisters started to make their way to Mum's stall, but Flame got waylaid at Batty Blenkinsop's bookstall next door.

Marina went to stand with Mum behind the bric-a-brac stall.

Ash stood, quietly, at the front of the stall.

Beeee-eeep! Ash looked around in alarm. Had anyone heard her stone? *Beeee-eeep!* it went again.

Mum was serving a customer and Marina was chatting to another. No one seemed to have heard it.

Beeee-eeep! it went again.

Ash felt something like electricity run through her body. Every sense was alert. Her mind started to race. In her pocket, the magic stone was vibrating.

What's it trying to tell me, she wondered. She looked at the stall. Either side of her, people jostled and picked things up. Mum chatted away.

Then she saw it. The magic box. The magic box sitting on the table, in amongst all the junk. The box that they had been looking for all week!

She picked it up carefully and held it out in front of her.

'I'll have this, please,' she said to Mum, holding out a pound coin.

'Okay, love,' said Mum, taking the coin and turning to serve another customer.

Ash took a few steps back and stood completely still. She stared at the small wooden box in her hands. It's like an old-fashioned cigar box, she thought. And she ran her finger around the pattern of the crossed circle on the top.

Then she tried to open the lid. It was locked. She glanced up and caught Marina's eye. Instinctively, Marina came to the front of the stall. She stared at the box in Ash's hand, then looked around to see if anyone had spotted them.

Suddenly Flame was beside them. 'What's up?' she asked.

'Look,' said Ash. 'Look what I've found.'

Flame's heart missed a beat. 'Oh my God!' she said.

Marina breathed out hard.

The three girls stared at the box.

Then, above them, a voice boomed. 'What have you got there, girls?'

Charles Smythson. Charles Smythson was standing right next to them, looking down at the box.

The Sprite Sisters gasped. Ash drew the box close to her. Charles groaned.

The girls stared at him. His handsome face was changing. It was as if had been wearing a mask that had now slipped. Behind the mask was an ugly face, an angry face. His face contorted, his eyes bulged, his fingers twitched, as he lunged towards the box.

'No!' said Flame, moving in front of Ash. Marina closed in on the other side.

'Leave it alone!' said Flame, sharply. 'Ash has bought it. It's *her* box!'

Charles struggled to smile. His hands seemed to be about to grasp the box, to clutch it in anyway he could, to push away the Sprite Sisters.

Behind the bric-a-brac stall, Mum had just finished serving a customer. She looked up and spotted Charles. 'Come and have a look at the bric-a-brac, Charles!' she called. 'It's all in a good cause.'

Charles turned. His fists clenched, he smiled at Mum. 'Hello!' he said, and walked to the stall. He struggled to speak coherently. 'Ottalie, the – er – the box that Ash, has – er – just bought . . . Where did that – er – where did it – er – come from?'

Mum glanced around. 'Oh, one of the cupboards at Sprite Towers, I expect,' she replied, breezily. 'I had a clear-out on Monday and took the things down to store at the Village Hall, in case Colin decided he wanted to keep them. They've been there all week.'

'Oh,' gulped Charles. He slumped. His body felt weary. His feet felt heavy. 'Monday,' he groaned. 'Monday – the day before I came . . .' Then he wandered off, staring into space.

Mum watched him go. 'Whatever is the matter with Charles?' she called to Flame.

'No idea, Mum,' she called back. 'Looks as if he's seen a ghost though.'

Flame turned to her sisters. They moved closer, huddled around the box, their faces tense with anticipation.

Flame began to feel her heart race. 'I think this is the thing we have to guard with our lives,' she whispered. 'Charles knows something about it – or why would he behave like that. Did you see his face?'

'Yes, he suddenly looked really mean,' said Marina.

'Do you think he'll try to take it from us?' asked Ash, drawing the box closer to her body.

'Yes, he may – but he must *not* take it,' said Flame. 'We must be on our guard. Ash, if he tries to talk to you, don't look him in the eye, understand?'

'What's happened?' asked Ariel as she bounced up, a blob of vanilla ice cream on the end of her nose. 'Why are you all standing so close together?'

Flame, Marina and Ash moved apart a little, to allow Ariel in. Ash pushed the box towards her.

Ariel stared. 'Oh my goodness! Oh my golly goodness!' she giggled. And she looked up at her sisters.

The tension diffused and the Sprite Sisters laughed. 'We've found it!' said Marina. 'We've found the magic box!'

'And tonight we'll look inside it,' said Flame. Then she stopped and looked around her. 'But not here – it's too public – and Charles is still around.'

She turned to Ariel and said, 'We've got to be very careful. Charles turned nasty and he tried to get hold of the box. We've got to guard it carefully.'

Ariel put her hand on Ash's arm and said, 'Don't worry, we'll make sure it's safe.'

For the rest of the fête, Ash walked around holding the box as if it were a matter of life and death. No one could take it from her. It meant she could not participate in any more games, but she was happy to watch her sisters.

'By the way, is your stone still in your pocket?' asked Flame.

'Yes,' replied Ash. 'Still safe.'

'And I've got George's letter and the key,' said Flame, patting her pocket.

Charles sat on a seat at the side of the village green and stared into the distance.

The box. It was here all along. What am I going to tell her, he thought. *What am I going to tell Glenda?* That the Sprite Sisters have beaten me to it? I can't tell her that. She'll string me out alive.

No, he thought, there's only one thing to do – and that's to get it off the girls.

Dark clouds gathered overhead as the fête began to wind down.

'Looks like we'll finish just in time,' Batty Blenkinsop commented to Mum.

'Thank heavens,' she said, looking up at the sky.

The Sprite family gathered around the bric-a-brac stall.

Charles wandered towards them.

'Hi, Charles,' said Dad. 'Good fête, eh?'

'Smashing,' said Charles, with one of his dazzling smiles.

'What's that you've got there, Ash?' asked Dad.

'It's a box,' she replied.

Dad laughed. 'I can see it's a box, love! Am I allowed to have a look?' He reached out – and there was nothing for it but to hand it to him.

The Sprite Sisters stood nervously as Dad turned the box over. Charles leaned towards it, his face tense.

'It's locked,' said Dad. 'But I expect we can open it at home.' He ran his fingers over the top of the box, traced out the line of the circle. 'Interesting,' he said, holding it up. 'Look at this, Ottalie – it's got the motif of the crossed circle.'

'So it has,' observed Mum.

'Did you get this from the bric-a-brac stall, Ash?'

'Yes,' said Ash.

'So it probably came from Sprite Towers,' observed Dad. 'There you are, Ottalie – shows at least one of my family appreciates our heritage!'

Mum laughed. 'Yes, dear,' she said.

'Mind if I have a look?' said Charles. Ash gulped. Charles smiled, charmingly, and reached out as Dad handed him the magic box. He looked at it from all angles, turned it over, then said, 'I should say it's nineteenth century.'

'Victorian?' asked Dad.

'Yes, probably around a hundred and twenty years old,' replied Charles.

'Ottalie, you've been throwing away our treasures!' Dad

burst out. He looked mortified.

Mum bowed her head. 'I shall take more care next time, don't worry.'

'Is it valuable, Charles?' asked Dad.

'Few hundred pounds, maybe more,' hedged Charles. 'We really need to find out what's inside though.'

'No!' said Ash, grabbing the box from his hands.

Dad and Mum looked surprised. Ash was rarely rude – or so attached to a thing.

'Kids, eh?' said Dad.

Charles smiled politely.

Thankfully, Grandma came up at that moment. 'I think we're ready to start clearing up,' she said.

'Yes,' agreed Mum. Then she looked at Dad and said, 'By the way, I've asked the fête committee and judges to come back for a drink when we're done here.'

'Okey-doke,' replied Dad.

For the next half-hour, Marina and Ariel helped their mother. Flame helped her grandmother clear the cake stall. Ash went with Dad to collect the vegetables, holding her box firmly under her arm. Charles hung around, helping a little bit here and there, but he sensed that the girls and Marilyn Sprite did not want him near them.

Then Mum said, 'Marilyn, why don't you take the girls home in my car, now. Colin and I have a bit more to do here. We'll be back soon.'

'Okay, dear – I'll go and get things ready for the drinks,' agreed Grandma, holding a pile of plates from the cake stall.

There was one more moment of danger on the village

green. Ash was standing alone by the big red car, when Charles appeared from around the other side.

'Ash,' he said, smiling down at her. 'Do let me have another look at the box – I'd love to see it more closely.'

Ash looked up, into his eyes – but he wasn't quite fast enough. She glanced away too quickly for him to use his magic power.

Blast, thought Charles. In the next instant, Ariel was standing beside Ash. 'Let's get in the car,' Ariel said, taking her sister's arm.

Charles stepped back and smiled as Marilyn Sprite walked past him to the car door carrying a box of crockery.

'I think he was going to take the box,' Ash whispered to Ariel, as they climbed in. 'I remembered what you said about not looking into his eyes.'

'It's okay,' said Ariel. 'You're safe now.'

On the short journey home, the Sprite Sisters told Grandma how Ash found the box and how Charles tried to take it.

Grandma listened as she steered the big red car around the winding lanes and down the drive to Sprite Towers. Raindrops started to fall on the window screen, as she brought the car to a halt in front of the house. 'Right, girls – you'd better stay inside tonight,' said Grandma. 'Apart from making sure the box is safe, we still don't know if the caravan is leaky.'

Then she turned around in her seat to look at her grand-daughters. 'Be careful, *please*,' she said. 'You don't know what's in the box and what power it may unleash.'

'Will you tell Mum and Dad about Charles?' asked Flame.

Grandma looked thoughtful. 'Charles has to complete the inventory and will be here for some days yet. I don't want to alarm your parents when we don't know what it is that he is really after – or why. Your parents think of him as family. It's a tricky situation.'

'Grandma,' said Ash, leaning forward.

'What, love?'

'Do you think that Charles knows Glenda Glass better than he's telling us?' said Ash, her big brown eyes wide.

Flame leaned forward and said, 'If Charles does know Glenda more than he says, it might explain how he knows about this box.'

Grandma nodded. 'Yes, possibly, but not necessarily. There might be records, somewhere in the family history, of this box. Perhaps it's valuable.'

Ash frowned. 'When Charles tried to take the box from me, his face changed – it looked really ugly. He reminded me of Glenda, when she was attacking the house. You know the way her face seemed to curl up and go all dark.'

Grandma sat up with a jolt.

'Ariel thinks he's got magic power in his eyes,' added Marina, leaning forward on the back of Grandma's seat.

Marilyn Sprite took a deep breath, her face deadly serious. She was silent for a few seconds. The Sprite Sisters waited, then she said, 'All right, girls, listen. That is what bad magic looks like. Charles must be a bad Sprite and he may well be working for Glenda.'

There was a shocked silence. Then Flame said, 'So what do we do?'

Grandma gazed out at the rain, frowning. An idea was forming in her mind. Finally, she turned back to them and said, 'We have three options.'

The Sprite Sisters moved forward, alert.

'First, we tell your parents and ask Charles to leave,' said Grandma. 'Second, we keep hiding the box, be careful, wait until he goes and hope he doesn't harm you.'

'And third?' asked Flame.

Grandma looked around at her granddaughters. 'Third, we do option two, but we also turn the tables. We string Charles along, to find out what he knows about Glenda.'

'I go for option three,' said Flame, immediately.

'That's because you are impetuous,' smiled Grandma.

Flame looked miffed. 'No, it's because I think it's the best plan,' she said.

Grandma nodded. 'Okay.'

'I vote for option three,' said Marina.

'And me,' said Ash.

'And me,' said Ariel.

'It's a risk,' warned Grandma. The Sprite Sisters looked at her, noted the sudden sharpness in her voice. 'I'm serious. You must be on your guard the whole time.'

They nodded, silent.

'And don't let Charles get his hands on that box,' said Grandma. She reached for the door handle and said, 'Now we must go in – our guests will be here any minute.'

CHAPTER EIGHT

THE
MAGIC BOX

'COME IN,' said Dad, standing in the open front door.

Batty Blenkinsop and his wife Virginia (who the Sprite Sisters called 'The Gargoyle'), Betty Carruthers and the other members of the village fête committee walked into the hallway of Sprite Towers, brushing the rain off their shoulders.

'Shame we can't sit outside this evening,' mused Dad. 'We'll have drinks in the drawing room.'

'We were jolly lucky the rain held off as long as it did,' said Batty.

The fête committee sat down in the drawing room, while Dad poured everyone a drink.

'Girls, please come and say hello to everyone,' said

Mum, as she walked through from the kitchen carrying a plate of canapés. 'Hello, Charles,' she said, seeing him coming in the front door. 'Come and have a drink with us.'

'Thanks, Ottalie,' he replied. He turned to look at the Sprite Sisters and noted that Ash was no longer holding the box. As he greeted the fête committee, his mind was racing to work out where Ash would have put it and whether he would be able to get it that evening.

I've got to be bold, he thought. I must take the first opportunity I get . . .

And there it was: an opportunity. Ash caught his gaze, then walked out of the drawing room. A minute later, Charles got up – and walked out too. For a moment, he stood at the bottom of the wide mahogany staircase, wondering if she had gone upstairs. Everyone else was still in the drawing room.

Quickly, Charles mounted the staircase to the second floor. As he rounded the corner, Ash came out of her bedroom.

'Ash!' he smiled. 'I'd love to have a closer look at that box.'

She looked up at him with her clear brown eyes – and held his gaze. In an instant, she was frozen by his power – and stood, immobilised, in the doorway. Charles moved past her into the room, without stopping to remove her memory.

For a moment, he stood there, in the middle of the room, his back to the open door. I wonder where's she's put it, he thought.

Suddenly, his feet seemed to have lifted off the ground.

'Whoa!' he cried, his arms jerking wildly. He was rising – rising up in the air, floating above the carpet. He looked down. His feet were now half a metre off the carpet.

Then a child's voice behind him, 'Remove the magic you have put on my sister, Charles, or I'll make you hit your head on the ceiling.'

His arms flailed in the air like paddles as he felt himself getting higher and higher. Then, just as his head nearly touched the ceiling, he dropped suddenly – then up, up he went again. Then down, then up. 'Argh!' he cried, beginning to feel distinctly seasick. He tried to turn his head – and managed to see who was behind him.

Ariel Sprite's face was like thunder. In front of her, she held up her right hand, her index finger pointed at him. 'Say something to Ash, Charles – *now!*' she shouted. '*Bring my sister back!*'

Charles tried to steady himself, but Ariel moved her finger and he wobbled again, as if his feet were slipping on a sliding floor. He was going to be sick any minute. How would he explain that to Ottalie and Colin?

'Okay, okay!' he shouted.

'*Go on – now!*' shouted Ariel.

'Ash, wake up!' Charles shouted.

Still standing in the doorway, Ash Sprite blinked. 'What happened?' she asked – then saw Charles hovering in mid-air. 'Oh, my goodness!' she giggled. 'Ariel, what are you doing?'

Ariel let her hand flop – and Charles Smythson dropped to the floor like a stone. As he lay, groaning on the carpet,

Ariel grabbed Ash's hand and led her along the corridor to her bedroom. The two youngest Sprite Sisters shut the door of Ariel's pink room, then went to sit on her bed.

'Are you okay, Ash?' asked Ariel.

'Yes. It was really weird. What happened?'

'It was just as Flame said it would be,' Ariel said. 'Charles used his dark power to hypnotise you. You were standing there as if you'd been frozen. I followed him in – just like we planned. He didn't hear me – I took off my shoes when I came up the stairs and crept in really quietly.'

'It was a good plan,' said Ash. 'Now we know for sure that Charles has magic power and how he uses it.'

Ariel stroked her sister's tufty chestnut hair. 'How are you feeling now?'

Ash nodded. 'A bit spacey, but okay.'

'We'd better go down,' said Ariel. 'Flame and Marina will be worried if we don't come back soon. They thought Mum and Dad would notice if we all disappeared at once. And we must tell Grandma as soon as we can.'

Very quietly, Ariel opened her bedroom door a fraction and peered through the crack. The second-floor corridor was still and quiet.

'He could still be up here,' whispered Ash, behind her.

'The way he fell, he's more likely to want to go down and have a large drink,' Ariel giggled.

'You do realise he'll know *you* have magic power now, don't you?' Ash said quietly.

Ariel turned to her sister. 'Ash, he knew that anyway. We all agreed it would be the only way that we could find out how to protect ourselves against his power. He's a Sprite – a bad Sprite – and he seems to know all about us. What we have to work out now is how he knows and why.'

She turned once more to look through the crack in the door. 'Okay, all clear – let's go.'

The two young Sprite Sisters hurried along the corridor and down the wide mahogany staircase. At the bottom, Ariel put on her shoes, just as Mum came out of the drawing room.

'Oh, there you are – they won't be much longer in there,' she smiled. 'I expect you're all getting hungry.'

'Where's Charles?' asked Ariel.

'Oh, he left rather suddenly a few minutes ago,' replied Mum. 'Said something about a headache.'

That night the Sprite Sisters climbed into their own beds. Mum came around to each of them. 'It's felt very empty in the house without you,' she said as she hugged and kissed each of them goodnight.

As soon as Mum had gone downstairs, Marina, Ash and Ariel crept along the corridor to Flame's bedroom. Flame crouched down on the dark navy carpet and pulled out a number of big books from the bottom bookshelf. Hidden behind these, against the wall, was the magic box. They had given a solemn promise to Grandma that they would keep it safe.

The four Sprite Sisters huddled together on Flame's bright red duvet cover. They had been itching for this moment since they found the box at the fête. Ash laid the box on the bed. 'Where's the key?' she asked.

'In here,' replied Flame, pulling George Sprite's envelope out of her dressing gown pocket. She reached inside the envelope, drew out the little key and handed it to Ash.

The four sisters fizzed with excitement.

'I can't sit still,' giggled Ariel.

'Come on, Ash!' said Flame.

'All right, all right!' replied Ash, as she pushed the little key into the little keyhole.

The Sprite Sisters held their breath as Ash turned the key, then gently opened the lid of the box. They moved closer and peered in.

'What's in there?' asked Marina.

Ash reached in and took out a dried rosebud. There were three others in the box. 'They must be from Sprite Towers,' murmured Flame. 'One for each of us.'

'It's so sad to think George didn't come back,' said Marina.

'He must have loved the house and garden,' said Flame.

Ash lifted out the dried rosebuds one by one and laid them carefully on the duvet, then looked back in the box. 'Look at this,' she said and held up an old black and white photograph.

The Sprite Sisters stared at an image of a formal family group. Some of them looked at the camera, others looked away. One little girl looked directly at it, with a piercing gaze. In the middle of the group, sitting bolt upright, sat the parents. Around them stood six children. All of them were dressed in old-fashioned clothes.

'I think it may be Sidney and Mim and their children,' said Flame, peering at the photograph. 'Yes, look – that must be George, standing at the side. He looks like the young man in the portrait.'

'He looks about twelve years old there,' said Marina.

'Who's the girl staring directly at the camera?' asked Ariel.

'I have no idea,' said Flame. 'But she feels sort of familiar.'

'The older boy behind them must be Fred, our great-grandfather,' said Ash.

'And the other boy and the two little girls?' asked Ariel.

'I am pretty sure Grandma told me Sidney and Mim had five children,' said Flame.

'Yes,' agreed Ash. She turned to Flame. 'So when was this photo taken, d'you reckon?'

'Well, George said in his letter he'd be nineteen when he went back to the Front in 1917,' said Flame. She thought for a moment, making calculations in her mind. 'So he would have been born in 1898. He looks about twelve here – so it would make it . . . 1910.'

'Wasn't that the year Sidney built Sprite Towers?' said Marina.

'Yes, you're right,' agreed Flame.

'This must have been taken in the summer – see the rose bushes in the background,' said Marina.

'The summer of 1910,' said Flame. 'Maybe they'd just moved in.'

'What's *that*?' asked Ariel, pointing. The girls had been so busy looking at the photograph, they had not noticed the piece of folded paper that lay in the bottom of the box.

'Careful,' said Flame, as Ash lifted it out. With great care, she unfolded the piece of heavy white paper and laid it on the bed between them. All over the paper were marks and scribbles drawn in ink. There were lots of lines and numbers and symbols going in all directions. The writing was scratchy and hurried, and in the same hand as the letter.

'It looks like George's writing,' said Flame. 'This must be the thing that George told us to guard with our lives. This is the thing that can unlock the secret of the towers.'

Marina, Ash and Ariel moved closer. 'What is it?' asked Ariel.

Flame studied the drawings. 'It looks like a series of floor plans – like Dad's architectural plans,' she said. 'I think it may be the five floors of Sprite Towers.'

'That looks like a floor plan of one of the towers,' said Marina, pointing.

'Yes, and that looks like a plan of the attics – look, see the winding staircases at either end of the corridor that lead up to the towers,' said Flame.

'That's the second floor, here,' said Ash, pointing to a third plan.

'Yes – there are our bedrooms,' agreed Flame.

'So that's the first floor,' said Marina, pointing to the bottom left-hand side of the paper. 'And *that's* the ground floor.'

'What's that dotted line?' asked Ariel, pointing to a line that ran across the East Tower.

Her sisters peered at the line.

'And those numbers and squiggles,' continued Ariel. 'What are they?'

'Let's see if there's anything on the back,' said Ash, turning over the paper.

The Sprite Sisters stared.

'Oh my goodness – it's the crossed circle again,' said Flame. 'If we understand the significance of that, we may be able to find the secret of the towers. So where do we start . . .'

'Let's go back to the plans,' suggested Ash. 'Let's go over them one by one and see if we can find something that connects them.'

'Look for the things that are similar in each plan, you mean,' said Marina.

'Can we use our magic powers to help us?' asked Ariel.

Flame grinned. 'No, I think this calls for brain power.'

'So what can we see in each plan?' said Ash.

'There's a sign for north – look,' said Ariel, pointing to a tiny *N* within the walls of the plan of the ground floor.

'You're right,' said Flame. 'There's another tiny *N* on the first-floor plan there. What about the second-floor plan?'

'Yes, look it's here – it's bang in the middle of the house at the front,' said Ash, pointing.

'And there's the one for the attics,' said Marina. 'Let's look for south.'

Sure enough, a small *S* was drawn on the south side of the house inside of the sections.

Within another minute, the Sprite Sisters had established that the letters *E*, *S*, *W* and *N* were written on each of the five plans.

Flame sat back. 'You know, usually on plans, you just get the *N* marked for north. You don't usually see all four directions marked. I wonder if the fact that they've been drawn inside each plan is significant?'

'We could go and stand in the positions of the four directions tomorrow and see what happens,' suggested Ash.

'What would we do?' asked Ariel.

'We could each face towards the centre of the house and use our powers to join together across the space,' said Flame.

'Like making the Circle of Power, but spread out,' said Marina. 'Yes, I like the idea of that.'

'And when we've done that, maybe the crossed circle will make sense to us,' said Flame.

'It'll be dangerous walking about holding the plan with Charles about,' said Marina.

Ash nodded, thoughtfully. 'Do you think Glenda told Charles about the magic box?' she said.

Ariel piped up, 'I asked Sidney about that.'

Her three elder sisters turned to her. 'I thought he told you we had to work things out for ourselves,' said Ash.

'Well, I did work it out – and I asked him if it was right,' said Ariel, pointing her ski-jump nose into the air.

'And what did he say?' asked Flame.

'He said I was right,' said Ariel.

'Yes, but what had you asked him, silly?' said Flame.

'I told him that Glenda Glass had really frightened us,

because she stopped at nothing to hurt us.'

'Yes – and?'

'And that Charles Smythson was really beginning to frighten me as he'd used magic on my sister,' said Ariel. 'I told Sidney that Charles was acting like Glenda – you know the way her face changes. Well, I saw that in him at the fête. He looked just like her. I asked Sidney what that meant.'

Her sisters nodded.

'And then, as I was talking to Sidney, I saw something in my mind,' said Ariel.

'What?' they asked.

'I had a picture of a puppet in my head,' said Ariel.

'A puppet?' said Ash, thoughtfully.

'So what did Sidney say?' asked Marina.

'Well, he didn't answer with words – but I got the picture in my head, so I thought that must be the answer instead,' said Ariel.

'Ah yes, of course – Charles is Glenda's puppet,' nodded Ash.

'And we may be in danger,' said Flame.

For a few seconds, the Sprite Sisters were silent, each thinking on this. Then Ash said, 'How are we going to keep George's plan hidden? We can't take the box everywhere – and, even if we did, he may sneak up on us and use his powers to hypnotise one of us again. Sooner or later, he's bound to get hold of it.'

'Somehow we have to find a way to keep it out of Charles's hands and to find the secret of the towers,' said Flame. 'We'll keep the box behind the books in my room, but carry the plan with us. I can tuck it down my front. Ash, you keep the letter and stone in your pocket.'

'I heard Charles tell Dad that he's going to be here till the end of next week,' said Marina. 'He said it would take that long to complete the photography.'

'Our cousins will be here on Friday,' said Ash. 'If we want to find out the secret of the towers before then, we're going to have to work very fast.'

'I wonder if there's a clue in George Sprite's letter?' said Marina.

Ash pulled the letter out of her dressing gown pocket and laid it out beside the plan. The four Sprite Sisters gazed down at it.

Ash read out, '*In the box is something very precious. Find it and guard it with your life. If you discover the power of the house, we may meet one day.*'

She looked around at her sisters. 'George wrote us this letter nearly a hundred years ago – how weird is that! How would he have known we were going to be born?'

'Yes, it's all very strange,' agreed Flame.

'And he says if we find the power of the house, we may meet him,' said Marina. 'That's even more weird!'

Ariel yawned and rubbed her eyes.

'We must get some sleep,' said Flame. 'In the morning, we'll go and stand in the four directions. We *must* find the power of the house.'

Marina, Ash and Ariel crept back to their bedrooms and climbed into their beds, and within a few minutes three of the four Sprite Sisters were asleep. Flame lay awake, thinking.

Downstairs in the room they called the snug, between the kitchen and the library, Mum and Dad sat together on the sofa watching a film.

Grandma sat in an armchair, with Bert curled up at her feet. She was staring at the screen, but she was not watching.

I hope I'm right about keeping Charles here to get information about Glenda, she thought. It could work in our favour, but it's risky and I don't like it. I don't like it a bit.

And the girls, thought Grandma. I wish I could protect them. But I have to let them fight their own battles . . . that's what Violet Duggery always says.

Two miles away, Charles Smythson sat in the drawing room at The Oaks, a tumbler of whisky in his hand.

Any minute the phone will go, he thought. Any minute.

As darkness fell, Charles got up and poured himself another whisky. He rubbed his head. I'll get my own back on those girls, he thought.

And yet, he thought – they are nice kids. Why am I doing this?

He sat back down in the armchair and stared into the dark. Money, he thought. I need the money.

The telephone rang. He took a large swig of whisky.

CHAPTER NINE

THE FOUR DIRECTIONS

CHARLES SMYTHSON woke on Sunday morning with Glenda Glass's voice ringing in his ears. All night long, her shrill tones had drifted in and out of his dreams. He had tossed and turned and had woken feeling weary and dull. Now he was sitting in the kitchen at The Oaks, drinking coffee and staring out at the big, leafy garden. Ominous grey clouds swooshed across the sky and there was the occasional rumble of thunder.

His mind was on Glenda Glass, however. When he had described to her how Ash had found the magic box at the village fête – and how he had missed it by a whisker – she was absolutely seething.

'You idiot!' she had screamed down the phone.

Charles had gritted his teeth. Glenda did not accept excuses. No matter that he had no way of knowing the box would be on a stall at the fête. No one could have predicted that in a month of Sundays.

In the box was something that Glenda wanted more than anything else. A plan, she had told him, a plan that contained the ancient magic of the Sprite family.

Glenda had always told him that her grandmother, Margaret, should have inherited this piece of magic, from *her* mother, Lily. Most of the magic that ran through the Sprite family had passed through the female line. But, instead of giving the ancient secret to Margaret, Lily Sprite had passed it to Sidney, her third child. He had used the ancient magic power and built it into his new house, Sprite Towers.

Charles was astute enough to see that, for the whole family's sake, Lily's decision was wise. By handing the secret to Sidney, she ensured that this bit of powerful Sprite magic stayed within the 'good' side of the family. Sidney was known to be balanced and kind, and he understood that magic should not be played with. From what Glenda and his father, Bernard, had told him, Charles understood that although Lily loved her daughter, Margaret, she could see a ruthless, ambitious side of her nature emerging at an early age.

Lily's great-granddaughter, Glenda, seemed to have inherited similar character traits, thought Charles.

What was certain was that the passing of the secret power to Sidney had caused a breach between some parts of the family. This might have healed had Glenda not been determined to have the secret power returned to her side of the family – and she would not rest until it was hers.

It was Glenda's obsession, but *she* had decided that it was *his* job to restore it to her.

Charles gazed out of the window, weighing up the situation in his mind.

Professionally things are going well, he thought. I've a good relationship with my cousin, Stephen – an extremely well-connected man who will help to further my career. I'm working on an inventory of Colin and Ottalie Sprite's family portrait collection, which will add to my reputation. I've completed the first part of this research and I've got five days of photography ahead of me.

That's all good, thought Charles, taking a sip of coffee.

However, the personal side of my life is not so easy, he thought. Glenda Glass is on my back and I haven't given her the information she wants. If I don't provide this information, she won't pay me – and then I will be really stuck. Added to that, I've exposed my magic power and been caught out by a bunch of girls. They'll work out a way to circumvent my power next time – and I don't want to have to use harsher magic on them. Still, I will just have to deal with that as it happens . . .

His mind drifted back to Ariel. That a nine-year-old girl could lift him with a flick of her hand – whoosh – straight up in the air: now, that was something. The discovery of her magic power could have benefits later, he thought. She had risked a lot to trick him.

He had known about the Sprite Sisters' magic before he

had come to Sprite Towers, of course. Glenda Glass had told him about the four sisters and how powerful they were when they worked together. She had also told him about the remarkable Mrs Duggery, Sidney Sprite's niece, who was now ancient, but whose magic was still incredibly strong.

He raised the mug to his mouth and took another swig of coffee, as his mind turned to Colin and Ottalie Sprite and the conversations they'd all had during the last week. What charming people they are, he thought. But, as bright and as sensitive as Colin is, he's not inherited the magic power that runs through the Sprite family. I could see it as soon as I met him and looked into his eyes.

He thought of Marilyn Sprite with her tall, dancer's body and her still beautiful face. She saw through me, he thought. I'd like to know what she thinks about Glenda Glass. Not a lot, from what he gleaned from Glenda; the old girl certainly seemed to have it in for Marilyn Sprite.

Charles stared at the big ash tree at the end of the garden. Glenda said the girls had sat in a circle to use their power, he thought. Four sisters with magical powers: I wonder what those powers are? If Ariel can lift, perhaps she has the power of Air? Fire, Water, Earth and Air. The power of the four elements? Flame would have to be Fire. Marina, the child of the sea – she must be water. And Ash – she'd be Earth.

Charles smiled. I wonder if Colin and Ottalie had any idea when they named their four daughters, he mused. They don't know about their powers – I can see it, he thought. I can see how elusive the girls are at times around their parents. Their grandmother knows, though. She protects them. They will tell her that I used my power on Ash – and then what?

Charles exhaled heavily. I'm not looking forward to this next week, he thought. Glenda's putting me under more pressure – and the Sprite Sisters have me cornered.

Glenda will stop at nothing, he thought. Every time I waver, she offers me more money and cranks up the pressure. Amazing the limitless funds that woman has, he thought. All that money . . . It must have come from her four dead husbands.

Not many people know all four husbands died, Charles considered. Even her son, Stephen, believes two of the husbands left after their divorces. Glenda's hidden her past well, thought Charles, but I have worked things out . . .

He frowned and rubbed his forehead with his hand. None of this would matter if I didn't need – and like – money, thought Charles. But I do like money. I like money almost as much as I like art. I enjoy my expensive lifestyle. I like the holidays and smart restaurants.

But those gambling debts . . . I must get rid of those quickly . . .

He clenched his jaw, decisively. Glenda's money funds my lifestyle, he thought. However nice the Sprite family are, I can't let her down. I need the money. Besides, she is not someone I'd want as an enemy . . .

Charles gazed out at the lawn. So what do I do, he thought. Do I go back into Sprite Towers and just act as if nothing has happened? Ignore the fact that I've used my magic power on Ash, and Ariel used hers on me? How do

I play it, he wondered.

As he stared at the trees blowing in the wind, a strategy began to form in his mind.

Yes, he decided, just act natural. The girls will have told their grandmother, but I doubt they'll have said anything to Colin and Ottalie. I will go in and get on with the work. I will stand back and observe the girls – let them have some space, let them think that I have backed off and lost interest, and that they are safe. Then I'll get to see what they do now they have the box.

The photography is going to be tough to complete in only five days, he considered. Everyone will expect me to be very busy. If, in the next few days, I am no closer to finding the truth about the power in the house – then I still have time to get the box and its contents for Glenda.

Charles smiled. It's a good plan, he thought.

And the photography: how should he proceed with that? I'll start at the bottom and work to the top of the house, he decided. That's the way. I have a feeling that this will tie in with the Sprite Sisters' plans somehow.

Half an hour later, Charles Smythson declined Ottalie Sprite's offer of a cup of coffee as he entered Sprite Towers. Instead, he began immediately, setting up the lights and umbrellas for the photography of the drawing room portraits. This, he decided, should keep him apart from Marilyn Sprite for the morning, at least.

In the kitchen, over Sunday eggs and bacon, the Sprite family chatted about the imminent visit of Colin's younger sister and her family. When Anne married Australian-born Geoff, she moved with him to Sydney and raised her family there. In a few days, they would be here at Sprite Towers for a fortnight's stay. The Sprite Sisters really liked their Aussie cousins, Jamie, Lottie and Daniel, and there was lively talk about the activities the family planned, including the cricket match next Saturday.

Cricket brought out the competitive glint in Colin Sprite's eye. He and his brother-in-law, Geoff, shared a passion for the game, and over the years it had become tradition at Sprite Towers to have a cricket match whenever the Aussie family visited. There was now much discussion about who to invite to play.

Mum had other things on her mind. As they got up to clear away the breakfast things, she said, 'Girls, don't forget you need to do some music practice sometime today. We've been a bit slack since we got back from France, but now you must get going again.'

'Okay, Mum,' they agreed. 'We'll do it this afternoon.'

The Sprite Sisters were itching to get going with their plan that morning, but Mum and Grandma asked Flame and Marina for some help in the kitchen. As usual, Ash went down to the vegetable garden with Dad, while Ariel was busy cleaning out her hamsters and gerbils in the utility room.

Every Sunday morning, Mum baked bread for the week. This morning, however, she wanted to make a bigger batch of loaves for their guests, who would be there on Friday. Marina helped her mother to mix and knead the bread. Meanwhile, Grandma and Flame made cakes and pies, some to put in the freezer.

'Anyone would think we're catering for an army,' mused Mum.

'We are,' smiled Grandma.

'There's one thing all the Sprites like – and that's their food!' laughed Marina.

All through the morning, Flame hoped to tell her grandmother about the contents of the magic box – but Mum did not leave the kitchen. Grandma knew something had happened and Flame knew she knew, but for now the details would have to wait.

At one o'clock, they all sat down to Sunday lunch of roast lamb and home-grown vegetables, followed by Grandma's rhubarb and apple crumble and custard. Charles stopped his photography to join them and commented on the delicious smells that had been wafting out of the kitchen all morning.

As they sat around the table, Mum and Dad noticed that Grandma and the girls were cooler towards Charles, and that he was slightly cooler towards them.

Once or twice during lunch, Charles's eyes met Marilyn Sprite's. He smiled, but he knew she had the measure of him.

Colin and Ottalie rattled on, asking him questions and talking about art and art history. Their enthusiasm helped to fill in any gaps in the conversation that otherwise might have appeared.

Afterwards, Dad carried the coffee tray out to the terrace to enjoy a brief moment of sunshine in an otherwise gloomy day, and they all followed.

As they walked out, Ash found herself alone near Charles. He turned and said to her, 'Ash, I'm so sorry I frightened you yesterday. It will not happen again.' It was said so quickly and so quietly that no one else saw or heard this communication.

Ash nodded and muttered 'Okay', and the next moment they were all on the terrace.

Ash sat there quietly. From time to time, she looked over at Charles and wondered what his intention was. Was he trying to tell her he would leave the sisters alone now? Ash mistrusted people who seemed to change suddenly: she judged them by what they did, rather than by what they said. So she remained wary – polite, friendly, but wary. Time will tell, she thought.

She watched the trees blowing in the wind and thought about how she and her sisters had hidden the magic box behind the books in Flame's bedroom, and how Flame now had the plan tucked into the front of her jeans and hidden by her T-shirt.

I wonder if Charles knows what we found in the box, thought Ash. She reached for the magic stone – there it was in her right pocket, safe and sound.

While Ash was deep in thought, Flame was getting impatient. The day was passing and the Sprite Sisters had not yet begun to find out how the magic plan 'worked'. Seizing an opportunity to have the ground floor to themselves for a short while, as the grown-ups drank their coffee, Flame thanked her parents and grandmother for lunch and went back inside. Her sisters followed.

Charles Smythson resisted the temptation to follow them. Don't panic, he said to himself. Everything will be fine.

In the hallway, Flame said to her sisters, 'We can't stand here with the plan. This is exactly where we need to be, but Charles will be coming in any minute. Let's go through to the snug.'

In the snug, they shut the door and kneeled down on the carpet. Flame pulled out the plan from her jeans and spread it out on the floor between them. The four girls leaned over and peered hard at it.

'Okay, look carefully,' said Flame. 'Last night, I thought about this plan – about the way it's laid out. I had the sense that George Sprite wants us to work in a sequence, floor by floor. Do you remember my dream the other day – about the rainbow of light that came out of the tower floor and went out through the wall? Well, I thought about that and had this feeling that the towers are where we're meant to get to – but we have to *start* on the ground floor.'

'Is this one of your "feelings"?' asked Ash.

Flame nodded.

'Okay, so where do you want us?' asked Marina.

Flame pointed to the ground-floor section. 'I've got to stand midway between the front and back of the house, on the east wall. According to the plan here, the *E* – for East – is at the far corner of the drawing room.'

'Where should I be?' asked Marina. She stared at the plan of the ground floor of the house, trying to pinpoint the tiny *S* written on the south side.

'The right-hand corner of the library, according to this – look,' said Ash.

'Ash, you're to stand in the corner of the dining room on the west side of the house,' said Flame.

'Yes, I see,' murmured Ash, peering at the tiny W.

'What about me?' asked Ariel.

'You're to stand just inside the front door, here,' said Flame, pointing. 'The front door is dead centre on the north side of the house.'

'Okay,' agreed Ariel. 'But how long have we got to stand in these positions? And how are we going to do it without Mum and Dad asking what we're doing, or Charles snooping about?'

Flame was about to answer, when Ash suddenly blurted, 'Charles apologised to me.'

'What! When?' her sisters chorused.

'As we were going out to the terrace for coffee,' said Ash.

'What did he say?' asked Flame.

'That he was sorry he frightened me,' said Ash, shrugging her shoulders.

'He wants us to think it's all okay and that he'll leave us alone,' said Flame.

'To put us off the scent,' said Marina.

'Yes,' agreed Flame. 'But we should be every bit as careful as before. We're stuck with him here till the end of the week, but we have to find the secret of the towers before our cousins arrive. All we can do is be very, very careful.'

'Will somebody please tell me what we're supposed to

do when we stand in these positions in the house,' piped up Ariel.

'Pumpkin, you're to stand still in front of the door and face towards the middle of the house,' said Flame. 'Then you're to direct your power to the middle of the house.'

'Shall I use my hands?'

'You could do – but I think we've got to see how we each feel,' said Flame. 'It may be something we do with our minds, rather than our hands.'

'I think we should visualise our magic powers joining together and filling up the space of the ground floor,' said Marina.

'With blue light, like we did with the Circle of Power?' added Ash.

'Brilliant idea!' said Flame, smiling at them. 'Just like we made the Circle of Power – only this time we fill up the house with our power. We'll see our individual magic powers as a blue light and send it all around the ground floor, then we'll do the same thing on the first floor – and the others, one by one.'

'But what are we actually trying to *achieve*?' asked Ariel.

Flame sat on her heels, her back straight. 'I've a sense that if we four put our magic power into the house, floor by floor, by the time we get to the top we'll have created a lot of new energy at Sprite Towers – and that something will happen in the towers.'

Ariel nodded her head up and down.

'You look very serious,' giggled Ash.

'Well it *is* serious,' replied Ariel. 'It's very, very serious.'

They all laughed. But then Flame's face darkened. 'There's only one problem: how can we get started when Charles is photographing the ground-floor portraits today?'

Before anyone could reply, Flame suddenly said, 'Sssh!' Quickly she folded up the plan and stuffed it back into the front of her jeans. Just as she had done this, the door opened.

'Ah, there you are,' said Mum, smiling.

'We're just going off to the camp,' said Flame, standing up. 'We need to check it's all okay down there.'

'Okey-doke,' said Mum. 'Your father and I are going to give Charles a hand with the photography. See you later, then.'

Outside, rain splattered and the wind blew as they ran down to the camp. Marina opened the caravan door and they climbed in and sat down on their beds.

'Feels like ages since we were here,' said Ash.

'We've only been in the house one night,' said Marina. 'But I know what you mean.'

'It feels chilly in here today,' said Ariel, shivering.

Flame sat on her bed, glumly staring at the floor. Suddenly she exploded. 'It's hopeless!' she said. 'We're never going to get the house to ourselves for long enough to make this plan work! What the heck are we going to do?'

Marina, Ash and Ariel waited. A few seconds later, Flame answered her own question. 'I think . . . I think that we should try and do the ground floor in the night, when Mum and Dad are asleep.'

'What, sneak down?' said Ariel, her eyes wide.

'Yes,' said Flame. 'It's going to be the only time we'll have the space to ourselves.'

'Okay,' said Marina. 'Let's do it – let's do it tonight. Mum will want us to stay inside again in this weather.'

'And what about the other floors?' asked Ash.

'Well, we can't go to our positions on the first floor at night – Mum or Dad would be sure to hear us,' said Flame.

'Maybe we can work really quickly in the daytime, once we know what happens on the ground floor,' said Ash.

'That's what I'm hoping,' agreed Flame. 'Mum and Dad may go out for a while – and we're just going to have to sneak around Charles.'

'Are you going to tell Grandma?' asked Ash.

'Yes,' replied Flame.

The rain stopped briefly in the afternoon, and the Sprite Sisters made the most of it. They played on their bicycles, looked after their rabbits and guinea pigs and tidied up the camp. They collected some firewood in the Wild Woods, lit the fire again and sat under the windy, whooshy sky singing some songs and making music.

Before supper, Mum called them in to do their music practice and they worked hard for an hour, playing their instruments.

Standing in the hallway with his camera and lights, Charles Smythson could hear the girls playing in the dining room – and he was very impressed. Glenda had told him they were good, but even so, he was surprised. He stayed at Sprite Towers until late, working his way through the portraits on the ground floor. Then he packed up his things and went back to The Oaks.

As the younger girls went up for their showers, Flame managed to get ten uninterrupted minutes with her grandmother. The older woman listened intently and wished her luck.

Then the Sprite Sisters went up to bed, followed by Grandma, then finally Mum and Dad.

At three a.m., the alarm on Flame's mobile phone beeped on her bedside table. She sat up, instantly awake and switched off the alarm. Then she got out of bed, pulled on her dressing gown and pushed back the curtain a little. The air was cool. The sky was dark. *I hope we'll be able to see our way around*, thought Flame.

I wonder if Bert will bark, she thought, as she crept along the corridor to Marina's room, then Ash's, then Ariel's. A few minutes later, the four Sprite Sisters tiptoed down the stairs, down and down to the hallway of Sprite Towers.

'It's so dark,' whispered Ash, as they reached the bottom of the stairs.

'It's a new moon – there's no moonlight,' whispered Flame.

'I hope we'll be able to see what we're doing,' whispered Marina.

'Let's make sure Bert knows it's us creeping about or he may start barking,' whispered Flame.

The four Sprite Sisters crept into the kitchen, stroked Bert in his basket, then came out and shut the door behind them.

'Okay, off we go,' whispered Flame.

Ariel moved to the front door and stood like a statue in front of it.

Flame turned the handle of the drawing room door very slowly. It squeaked slightly. She stopped, looked at Ariel and made a face that said, 'Urgh!', then pushed the door open slowly.

Marina tiptoed around the dark hallway to the snug and turned the door handle.

Ash crept to the dining room. That door squeaked too, and she looked up at the staircase. Mum is sure to hear, she thought. Her hearing is as good as a bat's radar. Then she opened the door on to a pitch-black dining room.

With some shuffling and stubbing of toes, the three older Sprite Sisters groped their way around the furniture in the dark. Two minutes later, they had each moved into their positions.

Each sister faced towards the centre of the house. Each focused her mind and visualised the blue light that they had seen before when they made the Circle of Power.

And, as their power rose, each felt the ground floor of the house fill up with a lovely blue light.

How long they stayed there, they were not sure.

Their trance was broken by Mum's voice in the hallway. 'Ariel, what are you doing?'

Ariel was standing in front of the doorway, her eyes shut, her arms stretched out.

She gasped as she heard Mum's voice and opened her eyes. 'I was dreaming!' she said.

'It's all right, love,' said Mum gently, noting her youngest daughter had bare feet and that her hands were cold. 'Just come on up to bed.'

And, thinking that Ariel had been sleep walking, and that she was now in a state of shock having been disturbed, Mum led her, silently, up the stairs to her bedroom.

Ariel dared not say a thing. She wanted to burst out laughing. Instead, she kept her eyes open wide and tried to think of the most boring lesson she'd ever had at school, which was Mrs Crump teaching dates in history. Her eyes glazed at the thought of all those numbers.

Mum had her arm around her shoulders and looked down at her anxiously.

Flame, Marina and Ash crept into the hallway and stared up at the staircase. '*What do we do?*' they gesticulated to one another, not daring to speak lest Mum should hear them.

Flame whispered into each of their ears, 'Go as quickly as you can to your room – Mum will come and check on us as soon as Ariel is settled.'

The three older Sprite Sisters began to climb the stairs in the dark, following their mother and sister. The stairs squeaked and several times they had to stop.

On the second-floor corridor, Mum opened the door to Ariel's room and led her 'sleepwalking' child to her bed. As she did this, Flame, Marina and Ash tiptoed around the corner to their own rooms, shut the doors, leaped into their beds and pulled the duvets over them. When Mum opened the door to each of their bedrooms, she saw them lying in their beds. What she did not know was that they were wide awake and shaking with laughter.

At the top of the second-floor staircase, Mum stopped and looked around. She had the sense that all was not quite what it seemed. Why was Flame's dressing gown in a heap in the middle of her bedroom floor, she wondered, and the curtain open slightly? I don't remember seeing it like that when I said goodnight to her earlier.

Downstairs in the big hallway, the grandfather clock chimed four o'clock. Mum leaned on the mahogany banister as she walked down the stairs to her bedroom.

'What's up?' asked Dad, blearily, as she climbed into bed beside him.

'Ariel was sleepwalking,' she said, quietly.

'She's never done that before,' he yawned.

'No,' agreed Mum, pulling the duvet over her. 'She was standing in front of the front door with her arms out. She was freezing cold – must have been there some while.'

'She's fine, love,' said Dad, snuggling up.

'Don't say anything to her,' whispered Mum, but he was already asleep.

Up on the second floor, despite the excitement, the Sprite Sisters drifted quickly to sleep. As dawn broke, the blue light that had filled the ground floor of the house a few hours earlier gradually faded away.

CHAPTER TEN

BUILDING THE LIGHT

THERE WAS much giggling when the Sprite Sisters woke –
quite late – on Monday morning.

They sat on Flame's bed, while Ariel described how
Mum had led her back upstairs, convinced that she was
sleepwalking. She mimicked how she had walked with her
eyes wide open, trying not to laugh.

As she walked downstairs that morning, Grandma felt a
sense of lightness, a change in the air. I wonder what the
girls have done, she thought.

Dad had left early for the office, and, over breakfast, Mum
expressed surprise that none of her daughters had appeared.
She told Grandma about Ariel's sleepwalking. The older
woman listened, concerned, and hoped they were safe.

At nine o'clock, when Charles Smythson arrived, he, too, felt a change in the atmosphere of Sprite Towers. He was standing in the hallway, looking around him and thinking about this, as Mum walked through.

'Morning, Charles,' she said, cheerily.

'Morning, Ottalie!' he replied.

Mum walked past him to the wide mahogany staircase. 'I'm just going to see where the girls have got to – none of them are up yet.'

Charles stood in the middle of the hallway. What is it, he wondered. There's something here – I can feel it, he thought. And the box – where have they hidden that?

Mum found the Sprite Sisters dressing in their rooms.

'Sorry, Mum, didn't sleep too well,' said Flame.

'That's okay, love,' replied Mum.

Marina said the same thing – and so did Ash.

Mum was confused. Was it something they ate that kept them awake, she wondered.

'Morning, Mum,' said Ariel, brightly.

'Morning, love. Everything all right?' she asked, expecting Ariel to look tired.

'Yes, fine thanks, Mum,' replied her little blonde daughter. 'I'm just coming down.'

'Okay,' said Mum and she headed back downstairs.

'Everything all right?' asked Charles, as she reached the hall.

'Yes, thanks Charles – they'll be down in a minute,' she said. 'Where will you be today?'

'I've got one more portrait to do in the hallway, then I'll start on the staircase paintings and make my way up to the first floor,' he said.

Coming down the staircase, Flame overheard this remark. Blimey, we've got to be quick, she thought, no time to lose. She turned and ran back upstairs to tell her sisters to make haste.

A few minutes later, Mum disappeared into the dining room to give a piano lesson.

The Sprite Sisters came down the staircase and passed Charles in the hallway. 'Morning,' they said politely, but coolly.

'Morning, girls,' he beamed back, as if nothing had happened. They looked relaxed and happy: they usually did – but even more so this morning. What were they up to?

In the kitchen, the Sprite Sisters munched their breakfast as quickly as they could, at the same time telling their grandmother what had happened the previous night and explaining what they intended to do today.

Marilyn Sprite listened attentively. 'You'll need to be very quiet, girls,' she warned.

'How are we going to get around Charles?' asked Ash. 'He's in the hallway, so he'll see us go upstairs and know we're up to something.'

'We could use the back staircase,' suggested Ariel. 'Then he won't know we're upstairs.'

'Good thinking,' said Flame.

The Sprite Sisters went to the small wooden door at the side of the kitchen. Flame lifted the latch and opened the door. Then, one by one, they climbed the narrow, winding set of stairs that led right up to the attics. It was up and down these stairs, many years ago, that the servants – the people who looked after Sprite Towers and the Sprite family – would have gone to get to their bedrooms in the attics. At each floor, a small latch door opened on to the main corridor of the house.

When Flame reached the first-floor door, she raised the latch. One by one, they came out at the end of the corridor. They stood, silent, for a few moments.

'Where's Charles?' whispered Marina.

'He's down in the hallway – I can hear him,' said Ash.

The four girls waited, then Flame gesticulated. 'Take off your shoes.'

As soon as they were barefoot, she whispered, 'Okay, Ash, you go into the spare bedroom, here at the west side of the house. Stand on the left side of the fireplace.'

Ash nodded.

'I'm going to be standing opposite you in the little box room at the east side,' continued Flame. 'Marina, you've got to stand beside the window in Grandma's sitting room, at the south side. Make sure you open her door quietly.'

'Okey-doke,' whispered Marina.

'Ariel, you've got the most difficult place to stand, as you've got to be on the landing right over the middle of the front door – at the north side,' whispered Flame.

Ariel's eyes widened. The four Sprite Sisters crept forward

towards the wide mahogany staircase. Flame looked around the corner of the wall and down to the hallway. She caught a glimpse of Charles adjusting some lamps below, as he prepared to photograph a portrait. Then he moved out of sight.

Flame gesticulated to Ariel and pointed to the elegant landing that curved around the back of the staircase. 'You've got to stand in the middle, there,' she whispered.

Ariel screwed up her face. '*Charles will see me!*' she whispered. 'He's so close.'

'Not if you're careful,' whispered Flame.

'*But what if he does?*'

'Well, sit down on the carpet, so you're lower,' whispered Flame. 'If he does see you, tell him you were meditating or something. And don't stick your arms out this time!'

'Shall I crawl around on my tummy?' whispered Ariel.

'Yes,' agreed Flame. 'And keep close to the far wall.' She turned to look at her sisters. 'Do you all know where you're going?'

They all nodded.

'Okay, let's go,' whispered Flame. 'Afterwards, go down the back staircase and we'll meet in the kitchen.'

Ash and Marina crept off to their positions. Ariel crawled along the side of the banisters towards the north landing, keeping as flat on the floor as she could. Flame waited until she was sure Charles was out of sight, before crossing the top of the staircase. Marina and Ash were safely in their positions, as Flame tiptoed along the corridor to the east side of the house and into her position.

Ariel sat cross-legged on the landing carpet, with her back against the north wall. Below her were the front door and the wide hallway. She could hear Charles Smythson moving about below, adjusting lamps and umbrellas. He would only have to climb a few stairs and turn around to see her. She shut her eyes and rested her hands on her knees.

As each of the four Sprite Sisters began to focus their minds and send out their magical power, the blue light swirled around them. At first, it was a small blue haze, but soon it grew until it filled up the first floor of the house.

Downstairs in the kitchen, Grandma felt the sense of lightness again. She looked down at Bert and noticed his long, sausage dog ears had risen in the air – and stuck out like wings.

Oh, my goodness – even Bert can feel the girls' magic, thought Grandma.

In the hallway, Charles stood still and looked up. What's that, he thought, as he felt a new energy around him. He blinked as he saw a blue light wafting across the first-floor landing. Instinctively, he moved towards the staircase.

'Charles,' came a voice behind him.

He looked around. Marilyn Sprite smiled up at him quickly, then looked away. 'Please would you help me move the kitchen table – it's too heavy to move on my own.'

For a split second, Charles was tempted to use his

magic power on her – again – but Marilyn had looked away too quickly. Besides, Ottalie was in the dining room and might come out any minute. I must play the game, thought Charles. Those girls are up to something, but I'll have to wait.

'Of course,' said Charles, smiling.

Funny, he thought, as he followed Marilyn into the kitchen. I didn't see the girls go upstairs or hear them. One glance at the small wooden door ajar in the kitchen told him all he needed to know. They've gone up the back staircase, he realised.

Grandma caught his gaze and moved across the big kitchen to shut the door. Drat, she thought. I hope he's not in here when the girls come down again. Then she glanced over at Bert and was relieved to see his ears had dropped down.

'I want to clean the floor underneath here,' she said, moving to the huge oak table and grabbing one side. Charles took the other. 'You take three steps backwards, please, and I'll come forward.'

Together they lifted the table. 'That's fine, thank you, Charles. I'll give you a shout when I need to move it back.'

Charles looked across the kitchen at the little wooden door. Shall I wait here for the girls to come down, he thought, or shall I go upstairs and see what they're doing?

Grandma pre-empted him. 'I'm just going to make a pot of coffee,' she said. 'Would you like a cup?'

'Yes, thank you,' he replied, still staring at the door.

'Did I hear the word coffee?' said Mum, walking into the kitchen. 'Oh, Charles, I wanted to ask you about the portrait of William Sprite. Have you got time to have a quick look at it now?'

'Of course,' he replied.

'That's fine,' said Grandma. 'You go on – the coffee will take a few minutes.'

Charles groaned quietly to himself. It was as if there was a conspiracy, suddenly, between all these women. As he passed through the hallway to the dining room, he glanced up the staircase. The blue light had disappeared.

As Mum and Charles walked into the dining room, the Sprite Sisters reappeared through the little wooden door of the back staircase.

'Go on, outside, quickly – he's on to you,' said Grandma, shooing them out of the kitchen. 'Go down to the camp.' Then, 'Wait! Take these,' she said, handing biscuits and a large carton of milk to Marina.

The four girls raced over the wide rolling lawn. Bert lolloped along behind, his ears flopping up and down.

'The caravan looks lonely without us,' shouted Marina, as they ran towards it.

'Let's get the fire going,' said Flame.

Within a minute they built a new fire with wood they'd collected and stored under a canvas. Flame lit the fire and Marina warmed the milk in a saucepan.

Soon they were sitting around the blazing campfire, drinking mugs of hot chocolate and munching biscuits. Over their heads, the August sky was dull and the wind had dropped. Cool air blew gently through the tall pine trees in the Wild Wood.

'I wish this weather would cheer up, said Flame, looking up at the blanket of grey cloud above them.

'I wonder how many chocolate biscuits Mrs Duggery has eaten since we last saw her,' said Ariel, looking at the remaining bit of her biscuit.

'Thousands, I should think – it's nearly five weeks ago!' laughed Marina.

'I've never seen anyone eat so many chocolate biscuits!' said Ash.

'I wonder what she's doing,' mused Ariel.

'She'd be pleased with us,' said Flame. 'We've done what she said and gone to the four directions to find our power.'

'I wonder what she'd think of Charles Smythson,' said Ash.

'Not a lot,' grinned Flame. She sipped her drink, then said, 'We did well this morning. That was amazing.'

'The blue light came so quickly,' said Marina. 'It was like – *boooph!* – and it was there, all around us.'

'Yes,' agreed Flame.

'So what now?' asked Ariel.

'We'll do the second floor,' replied Flame. 'But that should be easier, as it's around our own bedrooms.'

'Then the third?' asked Ariel.

'That's right – the attics,' said Flame. 'After that, the towers.'

'Well, let's get cracking,' said Marina. 'Here give me your mugs and I'll wash them.' And using her magic power of water, she cleaned the four mugs and put them back in the caravan.

'The fire will be okay until we get back,' said Flame.

'Let's sleep out tonight,' said Ash.

'Yes, I'd like to,' agreed Marina.

Bert followed the four sisters, as they ran back over the lawn and into the kitchen.

Grandma was sitting in the Windsor chair beside the Aga, doing her Sudoku puzzle, with Pudding the cat on her lap.

'Where's Mum?' asked Flame.

'She's gone out for an hour,' replied Grandma, looking up.

'And Charles – where's he?' asked Marina.

Grandma pointed behind her. 'He's making his way up the stairs.'

'We're going up to the second floor, Grandma,' said Flame.

'I don't like the idea of Charles being here when your mother and father are not about,' said Grandma. 'I'll keep an eye down here.'

One by one, the four Sprite Sisters filed through the little wooden door and climbed the narrow back staircase, with Flame leading the way. As she got to the door that opened on to the second floor of Sprite Towers, she took hold of the latch and tried to open it as quietly as possible. It clunked loudly. Flame looked around at her sisters and made a face. 'Blast,' she said, pushing open the door. 'Hope Charles didn't hear that.'

One by one, the girls filed out on to the corridor on the west side of the house. Again, they took off their shoes.

Flame pulled out the plan from her jeans and spread it out on the floor. Marina, Ash and Ariel bent over it to look as Flame pointed.

'Okay, same positions: east, south, west and north,' she whispered. 'Marina, you're in your own room. Ash, you're in your own room this end. Ariel, you've got to creep around the landing again and sit in the same place as before. And I'm going to my room at the east side.'

'Where's Charles?' whispered Ash. 'I can hear him.' She tiptoed along the corridor and peered around the corner of the wall at the top of the staircase. Charles Smythson was moving his lamps up the stairs and was almost on the first-floor landing. Ash crept back.

'He's quite close,' she whispered. 'He's nearly on the first floor.'

'Okay, let's be quick,' whispered Flame. 'Ariel, keep down. I'll come and watch out for you before I go to my room.'

Marina and Ash tiptoed to their rooms and waited.

Flame and Ariel crept along the corridor towards the staircase. Flame looked down. Charles was staring at a large portrait on the wall beside the first-floor landing. Ariel breathed hard, as Flame waited. Then, suddenly, she gesticulated and mouthed, 'Go now!'

Ariel set off, crawling along on her tummy to the north side of the landing. When she got there, she sat up, with her back close to the wall. Flame made a thumbs-up sign to her, then crept across the top of the staircase towards her room at the east side of the house.

Two minutes later, the four Sprite Sisters sat in their positions and focused their minds.

And two minutes after that, the second floor of the huge old house filled up with the beautiful blue light.

Only metres away, Charles Smythson was kneeling down, wrestling with a plug that would not fit in a wall socket. When he looked up, he blinked in astonishment. The light! He put down the plug, stood up and began to walk, very quietly, up the staircase.

Downstairs in the kitchen, Grandma felt the lightness of energy that she had felt earlier that morning. She looked down at Bert. 'Oh my goodness,' she said, seeing his ears sticking out again like wings. Instinctively, she moved to the kitchen door and walked out to the hallway. At the bottom of the staircase, she looked up to the second floor of the house. Charles was standing on the second-floor corridor.

Grandma walked quickly up the stairs.

Charles looked left and right along the corridor. He turned right around and saw Ariel, sitting with her back to the landing wall. Her eyes were shut and she was smiling.

All around him the blue light wafted along the corridor.

'Charles!' Grandma's voice called him from the first-floor landing. He turned and looked down.

'Would you mind helping me lift the kitchen table back – I've finished now,' she asked, smiling sweetly.

'Just coming,' he said, staring at Ariel.

The youngest Sprite Sister opened her eyes in surprise – saw him and gasped.

He smiled at her. Caught her, he thought, then turned to walk back down the stairs.

'The girls seem to be playing an unusual game,' he said to Grandma, as he walked into the kitchen.

'Oh, they're very imaginative,' she said, looking away. 'If we could just move the table back, please.' She grabbed one side of the huge oak table. Charles grabbed the other.

'Whatever has happened to Bert's ears?' he laughed as they lifted the table.

'Good heavens!' said Grandma, feigning surprise.

'Well, if that's all, Marilyn, I'll be getting on – lots to do,' said Charles.

'Thank you,' she replied, but he was already out of the door.

When Charles reached the second-floor landing, Ariel had disappeared – and so had the blue light. He stood still and listened. Where are they all, he wondered.

In Ash's room, Flame, Marina and Ariel waited silently. Ash held her door open a fraction and peered through the crack. She could see Charles standing, looking around – and held her breath as he looked towards her door.

To the four girls it seemed like a long, long time until Ash turned and whispered, 'He's gone.' She turned the door handle as gently as she could, and pushed the door shut. On the staircase, Charles heard the lock click.

They're still up here, he thought.

The four Sprite Sisters huddled on Ash's bed, in her neat, green-painted room with its plants and books.

Ariel was distressed. 'He saw me!' she whispered. 'He

was smiling at me – and I had the feeling he could see the blue light. What are we going to do?'

She looked anxiously at her sisters. Marina put her arm around her shoulders. 'It's okay, Ariel, don't panic. I'm sure he didn't see the light,' she said, gently.

'I wouldn't have known he was there if Grandma hadn't called up,' Ariel continued. 'He was so quiet. It's weird the way he creeps about so silently.'

Marina, Ash and Ariel looked at Flame. She was chewing her bottom lip, a sure sign she was thinking hard.

'We have to decide what to do,' she said in a low voice. 'Our cousins will be here in a few days – and they'll be around for the rest of the summer holidays. We need to find the secret of the towers *now*.' Flame's green eyes were intense. 'However . . . if we press on now, we've got Charles Smythson to deal with,' she said, pensively.

She was silent again. Her sisters waited, each trying to work out what to do.

'Once the Aussies arrive, everything will be on hold,' said Marina. 'I think we should press on.'

'What if Charles manages to get hold of the plan before we've found out what the secret is?' whispered Ash. 'That would be awful!'

Ariel looked at her sisters, her grey eyes wide and worried. 'Glenda Glass will be back as soon as Verena returns from seeing her mother in Buenos Aires,' she said.

'Glenda Glass,' repeated Flame with a low groan. 'I wonder if we will ever be free of her. Charles is watching our every movement, but it's Glenda who's behind all this. She must have a big hold over him. I wonder what it is? If we could find Charles's weak spot, maybe he'd leave us alone.'

The Sprite Sisters were silent for a moment as they thought about this, then Flame said, 'You know that dream I had about the rainbow light in the tower?'

Marina, Ash and Ariel nodded.

'I think we should be guided by that,' said Flame quietly. 'We *must* find that light. We *must* find the secret. We mustn't let Charles Smythson stop us.'

'I think George would want us to carry on,' said Ash, picking up the letter once more and looking at it. 'We have to find it for *him*.'

'I agree,' said Marina. 'I think we should carry on.'

'What about you, Ariel?' asked Flame.

The youngest Sprite Sister nodded. 'Okay – let's keep going.'

'Are you feeling better now?' Flame looked at her kindly.

'Yes, but I still feel a little bit shaky,' replied Ariel. 'Charles gave me such a shock – and I'd already had Mum the night before.'

Marina hugged her sister tight and smiled down at her.

'You had the most difficult position, pumpkin,' said Flame. 'And you did really well.'

Ash looked up. 'Shh, what's that?'

They stopped talking. 'It's Mum – she's calling us for lunch,' said Flame. 'Better go down.' She got off the bed, folded up the plan, tucked it into the top of her jeans, then pulled her T-shirt down to cover it.

Ash folded up George Sprite's letter and put it back into her pocket. She touched her other pocket to make sure she had the magic stone. It was still there.

Ten minutes later at the lunch table, Charles Smythson regaled Mum with the story of how Bert's ears had stood out like wings. Mum refused to believe him. 'Don't be silly, Charles!' she laughed. 'Bert's ears are floppy! They can't stand on end!'

Charles raised an eyebrow at the Sprite Sisters, aware that they were squirming in their seats.

Ariel butted in. 'What's happening this afternoon, Mum?'

Charles smiled knowingly at this distraction, as Mum said, 'I'm glad you asked that, Ariel. I forgot to tell you, girls – so much to think about – I saw the McIvers in town this morning. Quinn and Janey asked if they could come and play tennis this afternoon.'

'What did you say?' asked Flame, sharply.

'Well, I – I said I thought that would be fine,' replied Mum, surprised at her eldest daughter's reaction. 'I thought you and Marina would be pleased! You love playing tennis – and you always seem to be pleased to see Quinn.'

Mum glanced at Marina. She was frowning too.

That's put paid to our plans for this afternoon, thought Flame, catching Marina's eye.

Marina grimaced back at her.

'Have you other plans?' asked Mum.

'No, Mum,' said Flame. 'Tennis will be fine.'

'Well, you'd better give the McIvers a ring,' said Mum.

'Can you take Ariel and me swimming then?' asked Ash.

'Yes, okay, love,' agreed Mum. She looked around at Grandma. 'Unless you'd like to, Marilyn?'

Grandma smiled. 'No, you go,' she replied. 'I've a lot to do with all the food preparation this week.'

'Yes, of course,' agreed Mum.

An hour later, Quinn and Janey McIver cycled up the drive and played tennis with Flame and Marina. Mum drove Ash and Ariel to the swimming pool. Grandma did more cooking in the kitchen, keeping as close an eye on Charles Smythson's movements as she could.

He continued with his photography, aware that Marilyn Sprite was checking up on him at regular intervals. Despite her tenacity, he managed to have a good look in each of the girls' rooms. He was determined to locate the magic box.

And he did find it – hidden at the back of Flame's book-shelf. It was unlocked. He opened the lid and pushed aside the rosebuds and photographs. Damn, he thought. Where have they put the plan?

In the kitchen, Grandma kept watch on the pantry door. As Flame left the house to play tennis – wearing shorts and T-shirt – she asked her grandmother to look after George's plan until she returned. Grandma took the plan and hid it in an empty flour bin at the back of the pantry.

While she was busy with the baking, Bert snoozed in his

basket and Pudding lay curled up on the Windsor chair beside the Aga.

Once or twice Charles came into the kitchen, but he did not go into the pantry.

As soon as the McIvers left, Flame and Marina went up to change their clothes. A few minutes later, they came back down. Grandma retrieved the plan from the flour bin and Flame tucked it safely in the top of her jeans.

Dad was home by the time Mum, Ash and Ariel returned. Charles was still busily photographing the portraits. Flame and her sisters went down to the camp. There they built up the campfire and sat around it as they cooked their supper.

'We've got one more floor to do before we reach the towers,' said Flame. 'One more floor before we find the secret of the towers.'

That night, before they went to sleep, Ash used her power of Earth to put some binding magic around the caravan. The Sprite Sisters did not think Charles Smythson would try and steal their plan in the middle of the night, but they all felt they would sleep better knowing that if he did try he would be stuck – unable to move, his feet tied to the ground before he ever got to the caravan.

The Sprite Sisters slept soundly. As the thin crescent of the new moon rose in the sky behind the Wild Woods, Flame dreamed again of the rainbow light in the towers.

CHAPTER ELEVEN

FOILING CHARLES

THE GIRLS woke very early on Tuesday morning. The air was cool as they pulled on their clothes and ran up to the house.

'No time to lose,' said Flame, opening the kitchen door. Bert woke in his basket, as the girls walked quietly through the kitchen. Flame lifted the latch on the little door to the back staircase. One by one, they began to climb the narrow, winding stairs.

Upstairs, in their bedroom, Mum and Dad were just waking as their daughters tiptoed through the house. In her room, Grandma was lying in bed listening to the *Today* programme on Radio Four. She liked to know what was happening in the world beyond Sprite Towers.

At the top of the back staircase, Flame opened the door on to the third-floor corridor – the attics. The latch made a loud clunk, which she prayed no one would hear. One by one the sisters climbed out. They stood on the corridor, silent. All was still.

Flame's face was bright, expectant. 'I can feel the power building in the house,' she whispered.

'So can I,' said Marina, looking around.

'Me, too,' added Ariel.

Ash nodded. 'It's very strong up here now.'

Then Flame whispered, 'Okay, let's go!'

The four girls crept along the corridor. Flame went to the East Room, where they had mended the roof and walls just a few weeks ago. Marina went to the Train Room on the south side of the house, which had a huge table and model train that Dad and his sister Anne used to play with, when they were growing up at Sprite Towers. Ash went to the room at the west end of the corridor, while Ariel clambered through the Dressing Up Room on the north side of the house. This room had a decorative round window and huge boxes of old clothes.

The Sprite Sisters sat down in their positions of the four directions, their legs crossed, their backs against the walls. They closed their eyes and once again imagined their power meeting in the centre of the house. As their minds focused and their power came together, the magical blue light began to fill the third floor of the house.

The sisters felt so peaceful that they stayed in their positions for half an hour. It was only when their tummies began to rumble, that they came to and met back in the corridor.

Down below, on the first floor of the house, Mum was singing in the shower. In her bedroom, Grandma brushed her chic strawberry-blond bob into shape and smiled at herself in the mirror.

Standing in his dressing gown in the kitchen, Dad was transfixed. '*Whatever* has happened to your ears, Bert?' he said. He bent his long legs and leaned down to stroke the little dog's horizontal ears. Good Lord, they're absolutely rigid, thought Dad.

The sausage dog trotted to the back door and waited. Dad let him out and watched as Bert lolloped off over the lawn, his ears standing out. He lifted the big kettle from the side of the Aga, filled it from the tap and put it on to one of the hot plates. Then he went upstairs to have a shower and get dressed.

Up on the attics corridor, the Sprite Sisters had finished creating the blue light.

'Back stairs again, I reckon,' said Flame. She followed her sisters down the winding staircase, into the empty kitchen and closed the door behind them.

The Sprite Sisters ran back to their camp, over the wide rolling lawn.

'Oh my goodness!' shouted Ariel. 'Look at Bert!'

The little dog ran towards them.

Ariel stuck out her arms and pretended to be a plane taking off. 'Come on, Bert – you can do it!' she laughed, making the revving noise of an aeroplane engine. '*We have lift off – brrrrrrmm!*'

Bert ran along beside her, as she hurtled across the grass, her arms stretched out wide. Her sisters watched, laughing.

'He must be picking up the power in the house,' said Flame.

'Yes, let's hope he doesn't lift off!' said Marina.

'Come on, I'm hungry – let's get the fire lit,' said Ash.

'Eggy bread or fried eggs and bacon?' said Flame.

'How about eggy bread and bacon?' said Ash.

'Yum,' said Marina. 'That sounds good.'

Ten minutes later, the four Sprite Sisters ate their breakfast sitting around the campfire. Bert sat beside them, waiting for a piece of bacon, his ears returned to their usual floppy state.

'So, today's the day for the towers,' said Ash, through a mouthful of food.

'Yes, today's the day,' agreed Flame.

'Wasn't the blue light amazing this morning!' said Marina. 'I thought I was going to float off the floor!'

'It's got more powerful as we've moved up the house,' said Flame, squirting tomato sauce over her eggy bread.

'Ahoy there!' shouted Dad, appearing at the camp boundary. 'Am I allowed in?'

'Put down your weapons, then you may enter!' shouted Ariel.

'I haven't got any weapons!' said Dad.

'Well, hold up your hands so we can see you come unarmed!' shouted Ariel.

Dad walked in, grinning, holding up his hands.

'Morning, girls,' he said. 'That smells good,' he said, looking down at the frying pan.

He leaned down and stroked Bert's ears. 'Glad to see you're okay, little chap.' Then he stood up and asked, 'Did any of you see Bert's ears sticking out?'

The Sprite Sisters made gestures to say they couldn't speak, as their mouths were full. Dad stared down at the dog again. 'Hmm,' he said. 'Very strange.'

'So what's the problem, Dad?' asked Flame, swallowing.

'Problem?'

'What do you want us to do?'

Dad scratched his head. 'Do? Oh yes . . . what was it?' For a second he stared into space. Then he said, 'It's . . . it's the cricket match. Yes, that's what it was. Flame, we need your friend, Quinn, and Pia's brother Vivek, to come and play for us on Saturday. Quinn's a star bowler and Vivek's one of the best fielders at Drysdale's. I want them on my team. We *have* to beat Geoff's team. It's a matter of national pride.'

'It's a family cricket match, Dad!' laughed Marina.

He shook his head. 'Even so, I need the best players I can find,' he said.

'You know, Dad, for a quiet, rather diffident chap, you can be incredibly competitive!' said Flame, grinning.

'And *you're* not, I suppose!' he scoffed. 'Anyway, when am I competitive?'

'When you play tennis,' said Flame.

'When anything about cricket is mentioned,' giggled Marina.

'When we're entering vegetables into the horticultural show,' smiled Ash, biting her lip.

'Humph,' said Dad, scratching his chin.

'But we love you anyway,' said Ariel.

'Well, thank you very much!' he chortled.

'And, yes, I'll call Quinn and Vivek,' said Flame. 'Whichever team wins the match, we'll all have a wonderful afternoon.'

'Absolutely! Well, have a nice day,' said Dad, turning to leave. He stopped, turned back and asked, 'What are you all up to today?'

The Sprite Sisters drew breath. Then Flame said quickly, 'We're going to have an adventure. We are going to discover new frontiers at Sprite Towers!'

Dad laughed. 'Right! Make sure you don't get lost. I need you back for the cricket match on Saturday!' And he walked back to the house, Bert trotting at his heels.

Fifteen minutes later, with breakfast cleared away, the Sprite Sisters sat on their stools around the blazing campfire.

'Right, so we all know what we're doing,' said Flame.

'Yep,' agreed her sisters.

'Then let's find the secret of the towers – and no more creeping. Today we make a noise. Today we confuse Charles Smythson!'

And they ran up to the house.

'Have you had breakfast?' asked Mum, as they came into the kitchen.

'Yes thanks, Mum,' said Ash.

'Okay – well go and have a shower before you do anything else,' she called to their backs.

Grandma was coming down the stairs. Marina, Ash and Ariel said, 'Morning, Grandma!' as they raced past. Flame stopped to talk.

'We've done the third floor, Grandma,' she said, softly.

'Yes, I can feel it,' she replied. 'Your father said Bert's ears were sticking out like aeroplane wings when he came down this morning. Poor Bert!'

Flame smiled. 'The blue light was very strong.'

Marilyn Sprite nodded, then gazed around. 'What are you going to do now?'

'The towers – today we do the towers,' said Flame, half afraid her grandmother would veto this. Instead, she looked her eldest granddaughter in the eyes and said, 'Okay, but be *careful*.'

Flame nodded. 'We will be, I promise.'

'What about Charles? He'll be here any minute.'

'We have a cunning plan,' smiled Flame. 'You'll see.'

At that moment, the front door of Sprite Towers opened. Charles Smythson called, 'Hello,' as he walked in, carrying his black notebook.

'Morning, ladies,' he said, with his charming smile.

'Morning, Charles,' replied Grandma, a little brusquely.

'Morning,' said Flame, but he didn't hear. Grandma and Flame glanced at one another. Charles was standing in the hallway, looking up and down, side to side, a look of intense concentration on his face. They both knew he sensed that the magic power in the house was getting stronger.

'I'm off,' said Flame. She ran up the stairs to join her sisters and have a shower.

The Sprite Sisters made a lot of noise that morning. They charged up and down the stairs – so much so that Charles got worried about his camera being toppled over. He was now working on the second-floor portraits and could hear them up on the attics floor. Someone was shouting something about a 'play'.

What*ever* are they up to, he wondered.

As he had walked in that morning, he knew they had been making more magic. There was so much energy in the house that he thought the roof might lift off. He had expected to find the Sprite Sisters creeping about. But no, they were charging around instead.

In the Dressing Up Room, the Sprite Sisters opened boxes and trunks and pulled out clothes and hats.

'I'm going to be a cavalier,' said Ariel, pulling on a huge hat, its wide rim curled up on one side. Several feathers swooshed out the back.

'You need long boots,' said Flame.

'And a sword,' said Ash.

'And a silk waistcoat,' added Flame.

Ariel started hunting through the boxes.

Marina held up a long, shimmery silver-beaded dress. 'Hey, this is cool – I'm going to be a flapper from the 1920s!'

'You'll need a headband and a feather boa,' said Flame.

'I wonder which Sprite owned this, originally,' said Marina, staring at the dress.

'Here's a pink boa – catch!' shouted Ariel, tossing it to Marina, who wrapped it around her neck.

'Where are the boots?' asked Ariel.

'In that box,' replied Ash, pointing to a huge wicker trunk at the side of the room. 'What's that?' she said, shuffling sideways behind a huge trunk and grabbing at a long pole with a huge ball on either end.

'They were Dad's dumb-bells – you know when he and Mum went to that fancy dress party and he went as a strong man?' said Marina, pulling on her shimmery dress.

Ash hoicked the dumb-bells out of the corner and held them high above her head. 'Good thing the weights are made of polystyrene!' she laughed.

'Why don't you dress up as a lady weight-lifter?' suggested Ariel, sitting on the floor and pulling up an enormous pair of leather boots.

'Yes!' said Ash enthusiastically.

'Here's a navy-and-white striped swimming costume,' said Flame, throwing it to her.

'And you must wear this!' said Ariel, throwing Ash a huge blond wig.

'What about you, Flame?' asked Ash.

'I need something I can put on top of my jeans, as I'm still carrying around this plan tucked into my belt,' she replied, patting it on her belly.

'Can you take George's letter, too?' asked Ash, handing it to her. Flame looked at the envelope, noted its now dog-eared corners and crumpled appearance, then put it into her jeans pocket.

'Flame, how about – how about being a Maharajah?' suggested Marina, as she searched for a pair of 1920s shoes in another huge box. 'You could have a wonderful turban and lots of colourful flowing robes.'

'How on earth are we going to make up a play about a cavalier, a flapper, a lady weight-lifter and a Maharajah?' laughed Flame.

'We'll think of something!' said Marina.

Within half an hour the Sprite Sisters were ready. Flame looked magnificent. She had tied back her hair and now sported a huge, colourful turban and a long, black stick-on beard. On top of her jeans, she had pulled on some wide, emerald-green silk trousers that gathered into the ankle. Over these hung several long flowing robes, including a heavily embroidered, gold-and-green brocade coat. Her hands dripped with jewelled rings. In her right hand, she clenched a large, silver-coloured sword, shaped like a scimitar – another one of Dad's fancy dress party creations. In her left, she held a small jewelled box.

'I am the Maharajah of Kanchacherrypelli!' she said, proudly. She made a deep bow to her sisters.

Marina slinked forward in her shimmery beaded dress. Her thick, dark curly hair had been pulled back into a low bun at the nape of her neck. Around her head was a silver-beaded band, out of which stood three turquoise-coloured ostrich feathers. Long ivory silk gloves went all the way up her bare arms. On her feet were original 1920s T-bar shoes made of soft ivory leather.

'I'm Loulou de Sylvesterpoms from Chicago,' she drawled in a husky voice and lowered her eyelids. 'And I can do the Charleston.' She held out her palms in front of her and turned them in quick circles, at the same time kicking up her legs behind her.

'I'm Mighty Masitchka, ze Strongest Woman in ze Vorld!' shouted Ash, in a Russian accent. Her huge blond wig tipped sideways as she swung the enormous dumb-bells over the head. Under the navy-and-white striped swimming costume, she wore a red T-shirt and bright red tights. She'd stuffed these with T-shirts to create huge muscles, which now bulged on her chest, arms and legs. Big white socks came halfway up her calves, and on her feet were a pair of huge brown, lace-up leather boots.

'A-ha – have at you!' shouted Ariel, thrusting a long, thin silver plastic sword at her sister.

Ash swung her dumb-bells at the sword and nearly knocked Flame over.

'Blimey, you two – be careful!' said Flame. She looked at Ariel. 'And who are you?'

Ariel pulled off her huge hat, stepped forward with her right boot and made a deep, sweeping bow with her right arm. 'I am the Duke of Flossington. I have very clean teeth!'

Her older sister laughed. 'Look at the size of your boots, Ariel! How on earth are you going to walk around in those?'

'A tiddling problem for a brave cavalier from His Majesty's regiment, I assure you!' said Ariel, making another low bow and almost falling over in the process.

For a few minutes, the Sprites Sisters giggled about their outfits, then Flame said, 'Okay, are we ready?'

Marina, Ash and Ariel nodded.

Flame smiled. 'Well, let's confuse Charles Smythson!'

For the next hour, the Sprite Sisters marched through the house. Ariel clomped about in her huge boots and Ash swung her dumb-bells, narrowly missing some of the lights. Up and down, in and out of rooms, sometimes together, sometimes separately, coming up the back stairs, then down the front – round and round and round they went. Every time they passed Charles Smythson on the second floor, he grabbed at his camera, just in case they knocked it over.

'Fiend!' boomed a loud voice.

Charles spun around to look down into the hallway.

'I command you,' continued the Maharajah to Loulou de Sylvesterpoms, by the front door. 'I command you to tell me where the treasure is!'

Whereupon, Loulou stepped back, held up her hands and screamed, 'If you kill me, the secret will die with me! I may look like a silly flapper, but my heart is made of steel! I will never, never tell!' At which point she fainted on the floor.

Charles turned again as Mighty Masitchka made a loud roaring noise and swung her dumb-bells over her head on the third-floor landing. At the same time, the Duke of

Flossington, said, 'Which sort of compost do you recommend for dahlias?' then tripped over.

Charles screwed up his face. What the heck are they doing, he wondered. They're all talking complete gibberish. He sighed. Peace and quiet would be nice, he thought. Time was pressing and he just wanted to get on.

Two minutes later, Mighty Masitchka and Loulou de Sylvesterpoms sauntered down the stairs, discussing the merits of purple glitter eye-shadow, while the Maharajah of Kanchacherrypelli and the Duke of Flossington had a sword fight across the first-floor landing.

'What are you doing?' asked Charles, as the Duke raced past him.

'Acting a play, of course! What did you think we were doing?'

Charles clenched his jaw. Ottalie and Colin were out. Marilyn Sprite seemed to take no notice of the hullaballoo – she'd not come out of the kitchen to tell her granddaughters to pipe down or tell them to be careful not to knock over his camera and umbrellas. He was trying to get the right angle on a particularly difficult shot – a portrait that they could not take down from the wall as it was too big to lift and which was hung quite high.

As the girls' noise continued unabated, Charles tried to concentrate. I've got to get this floor finished today, he thought. I must screen this racket out of his mind and forget about the Sprite Sisters.

The Sprite Sisters did not all disappear at the same time.

Rather, they made their way up to the West Tower one by one. The Duke of Flossington went first, whilst the Maharajah and Mighty Masitchka argued about the merits of ballooning in the drawing room, and Loulou danced the Charleston across the third floor.

As Loulou slipped up to the tower, Mighty Masitchka stood by the front door and appeared to lift a weight so heavy that she collapsed under it and lost her huge blond wig. She lay on the floor so long, Charles Smythson thought something had really happened to her – but next time he looked around Mighty Masitchka and the wig were gone.

Upstairs, there began an incredible booming noise, as the Maharajah walked along the second-floor corridor reading out loud – and very loud it was, too – Lord Macaulay's famous poem, 'How Horatius Held the Bridge'.

'*Lars Porsena of Clusium, by the Nine Gods he swore,*' boomed the Maharajah.

'*That the great house of Tarquin should suffer wrong no more.*

'*By the Nine Gods he swore it, and named a trysting day . . .*'

This is ghastly, thought Charles. I wish those wretched girls would shut up! I'm getting behind, he thought, anxiously. Now what should I do with the lighting on this one, he wondered, staring at a huge portrait of Arthur Sprite.

He was dimly aware of the Maharajah's voice receding up the third-floor staircase.

'And bade his messengers ride forth,
East and west and south and north.
To summon his array . . .'

As the booming faded away, Charles was oblivious to anything, except the wonderful quiet in the house. Quickly, he grabbed one of the umbrella lights and moved it into position and plugged in the electric lead. There's not a second to lose, he thought. Any minute those beastly girls will come charging back again . . .

Up in the West Tower, the four Sprite Sisters stood in the position of the four directions, still wearing their dressing up clothes.

At the east side, stood Flame. Beside her, opened out on the wooden floorboards, lay the plan she had been hiding.

On her left, at the south side of the Tower, stood Marina.

Opposite Flame, at the west wall of the Tower, stood Ash, minus her dumb-bells.

Ariel breathed heavily, as she stood on the north side. She lifted her hands in the air and stared into the centre of the space.

The four Sprite Sisters shut their eyes and focused their minds.

As they did so, the West Tower lit up in a blaze of bright blue light. The floor shook slightly and the girls wobbled. The blue light started to change colour – from blue to pink to white.

'Oh my goodness!' squeaked Ariel, opening her eyes.

'*Keep still – hold the power! Don't move your hands!*' said Flame.

And there, in the middle of the room, was what looked like the end of a rainbow. All the colours of the spectrum poured down on the bare wooden floorboards in a narrow arc of light.

The four sisters stared at the rainbow, their mouths dropping open in astonishment.

'It's the rainbow from my dream!' said Flame, her eyes wide with wonder.

Within the rainbow, the shape of steps began to form.

'What's happening?' said Ash.

'I don't know!' said Flame. '*Hold the power!*'

'There are steps . . . ' gasped Marina. 'Steps going up . . . '

'But where to?' asked Ash. 'Where do they lead?'

'*Hold the power, all of you!*' said Flame. 'Keep going!'

'The rainbow points towards the East Tower,' said Marina.

'It looks like a bridge!' said Ariel, her grey eyes round as saucers. 'It's a bridge pointing to the other tower!'

The Sprite Sisters stared.

Just then, Mum's voice called from the outside the door. '*Girls – where are you?*'

The Sprite Sisters gasped and dropped their hands. As the tower door opened, the bright light vanished, the rainbow disappeared.

Mum's head appeared around the door, 'Oh, there you are – I've been looking for you.'

Behind her stood Charles Smythson. He had followed her up to the tower aware, suddenly, that something was afoot and offering to help find the girls. His eyes blazed, as he realised the Sprite Sisters had tricked him again. He looked over the top of Mum's head.

I can feel the power in this room, he thought. What's happening?

Mum walked in and stood in the centre of the tower room, where only seconds before had been the rainbow of light. Charles waited in the doorway. Her daughters stood around the edge of the room, looking dazed. They were silent and made no reaction.

'Girls, are you all right?' said Mum, in a sharp voice. 'You look as if you've been hit on the head.'

'Yes,' answered Flame, quietly. The Sprite Sisters blinked, each feeling the light drain out of their bodies.

'There's a funny feeling in here,' said Mum, looking around the room. 'What have you been doing?'

Flame suddenly realized that the plan was still on the floor – in full view of Charles. She acted instantly, stepping sideways, so that her long robe covered it. But it was too late. As Flame looked up, she saw him eyeing it – then caught his glance.

Blast, she thought.

Mum asked again, 'So what *are* you doing?'

Marina leaped forward and threw out her arms like a seasoned 'luvvie'. 'A play, Mum! I'm Loulou de Sylvesterpoms, a flapper from Chicago!' she drawled. 'Here, on my left is Mighty Masitchka, minus her dumb-bells. She's the strongest woman in the whole of the western hemisphere – only she's having a day off. And this dastardly character is the Duke of Flossington, a loyal servant to King Charles II!'

Mum smiled as Ariel pulled off her hat, stepped forward and bowed her deep bow.

'And what's the play called?' asked Mum, brightly.

'It's – it's – we haven't got a title for it yet!' said Marina, smiling. 'But all will be revealed!'

'When shall we see it?' asked Mum. Marina drew breath – noticed Charles Smythson's smirk – and replied, 'Later!'

'Great!' said Mum. 'We look forward to it! Come on down now – it's lunchtime.' She turned and walked out of the room.

Charles moved to let her pass, then turned back towards the tower room. For a split second, he held Flame's gaze. His mouth turned up at one side and his left eyebrow lifted.

'I am very much looking forward to your "play",' he said. 'And I do hope that everything *will* soon be revealed.'

Then he turned and walked out of the door.

'Urgh – loathsome man!' said Flame, punching her right fist into her left hand.

The Sprite Sisters stood limp and exhausted. 'I can hardly lift up my arms,' said Ash.

'Nor me,' agreed Marina.

'It's as if the light has taken all our energy,' said Ariel.

'I don't think we were meant to finish like that,' said Flame, staring into the centre of the room. 'Mum bursting in like that broke the magic.'

She pulled herself up and drew back her shoulders. 'Take

a deep breath,' she said. Then she picked up the plan from the floor, folded it up and stuffed it into the top of her jeans.

It was not the first time the Sprite Sisters had sat at the kitchen table dressed up in outlandish clothes. Throughout lunch they managed to parry Charles's remarks and questions. Several times, Grandma came to the rescue and diverted the conversation – twice when Mum commented how odd the atmosphere in the tower had felt.

An evening performance of the play was promised. Charles smiled and said, 'Well, you have certainly had some lively rehearsals this morning. It looks to be a multi-layered plot.' He turned to Flame and asked, 'Is there a script?'

'No, Charles,' she smiled, icily. 'We keep it all in our heads. If you write something down, it might get stolen.'

'Absolutely!' replied Charles, his white teeth gleaming. Then he added, with a glint in his eye. 'Well, I'm impressed. I think you've all been very clever.'

'Yes,' smiled Flame. 'We have!'

After lunch, the Sprite Sisters took off their outfits, put on their jeans and T-shirts, tidied up the Dressing Up Room and walked back down to the camp.

There they lay on their beds in the caravan, exhausted.

'So what is this rainbow?' asked Ariel. 'There were steps, remember? Where do they lead?'

No one answered.

Ash stared up at the ceiling. Then she said, 'I wonder if it could be some kind of portal?'

Flame, Marina and Ariel turned their heads to look at her – then all sat up, a look of excitement on their faces.

'A portal?' said Flame.

'Yes, you know – a doorway to another world or time,' said Ash, pulling herself up on her elbow.

'Fab-fantasic!' said Ariel. 'A portal! Wow!'

'A *portal . . .*' Flame repeated, thinking hard on this idea.

'Could *this* be the secret of Sprite Towers?' said Marina, her face incredulous. 'A portal?'

She looked around at her sisters. 'It could explain why George Sprite wrote to us from the past.'

'How?' asked Flame, in her analytical way. 'Why?'

'Well, maybe George can move through time,' said Marina. She was silent for a few seconds, then added, 'Maybe he wants to meet us.'

Ariel gaped in amazement. 'What – like a *ghost*?'

'He wouldn't be a ghost if the portal took us to his own time,' said Flame, thoughtfully. 'He'd probably look how he always did.'

Ariel looked very relieved at this, then Ash said, 'In his letter, George said something about other people trying to get hold of the secret – and that he and his father had stopped them.' She was silent for a moment, then added, 'I wonder if the portal is something *we* can open, as we have the powers of the four directions?'

Flame looked at her. 'Yes, I was just thinking that.'

'So what do we do?' asked Ariel, jumping up.

'Ariel, sit down!' said Flame, sharply. 'Listen, you are

not to mess about with this!' Grandma is right about taking care. We don't have a clue yet what this is about.'

Ariel sat back down on the bed, as Marina said, 'Nevertheless, we had better get going – given the Aussies will be here in three more days.'

'How on earth are we going to get enough time alone, in the tower, with Charles snooping about?' said Ash. 'It's tricky enough trying to dodge Mum and Dad!'

'And Charles knows what we're up to – he'll watch out for us to going into the towers,' added Flame. 'We can't use the play ruse again.'

'We could go up there at night,' suggested Ariel.

Flame, Marina and Ash stared at her, their mouths open.

'What's the matter? Why are you looking at me like that?' said Ariel. 'Night is a good idea. Charles won't be here and Mum and Dad will be asleep. We can get in and out at the kitchen door – or sleep inside. That's probably easier. Let's do it tonight.'

She smiled brightly at her three sisters, then said, 'You look like goldfish.'

Flame, Marina and Ash closed their mouths.

Flame exhaled long and slow. 'Phew . . . I don't know . . .' she said. 'You want us to open up the portal tonight? Hmm . . . it could be very risky.'

'There's no reason it would be any more risky at night, than in the day,' said Ash. 'I'm not sure portals go by the clock. But, as Ariel says, it would mean we'd have the place to ourselves – and that has to be a good thing.'

Flame chewed her lip. 'We don't have to do this,' she said.

'*Yes, we do!*' said her three sisters.

'Come on, Flame! We can't let George down!' said Ash.

'What's the problem?' asked Marina. 'You're not usually like this.'

Flame shook her head. 'I don't know. I just have a bad feeling about it.'

'But we won't have a minute to ourselves!' said Marina. 'You know what it's like when all the family are here!'

Flame nodded reluctantly at her. 'Yeah!'

'So we do it tonight?' said Ariel.

Marina, Ash and Ariel looked at Flame.

She bit her lip, then nodded. 'Okay – tonight, then.'

'We've got to do our play after supper,' said Ash.

'Urgh – yes, I'd forgotten that,' said Flame. 'We'll have to plan it this afternoon. Let's rest now. We're going to need all our energy tonight.'

And for the next hour, the four Sprite Sisters snoozed on their bunk beds, as the wind whistled through the Wild Woods.

CHAPTER TWELVE

HELP!

THAT TUESDAY evening, the Sprite Sisters performed their play in the drawing room, in front of Mum and Dad, Grandma and Charles Smythson. *The Curse of the Lavender Diamond* was acted with great gusto. Its labyrinthine plot moved across several time periods and continents, connecting a seventeenth-century English soldier with an eighteenth century Indian Maharajah and a 1920s American flapper, who was trying to escape the Mob. A Russian lady weightlifter with a crazy blond wig came to the rescue and saved the diamond.

Everyone laughed and had fun.

Several times during the evening, Mum and Dad commented on the lovely warm atmosphere in the house. But since neither of them knew about magic, they put the feeling down to the sheer enjoyment of being together.

As the evening drew to a close, the Sprite Sisters went up to bed in their own rooms. Charles Smythson said goodnight and drove back to The Oaks. Mum, Dad and Grandma sat for a while, talking.

In the drawing room of Stephen Glass's country house, Charles poured a tumbler of whisky and sat down in a big cream armchair. He stared into space as he took a mouthful of the fiery liquid. It had been a long, tiring day, in which he had done a considerable amount of photography – and he had worked hard, despite the Sprite Sisters' interruptions.

Then there had been the girls' play to sit through this evening. Now he just wanted to go to bed and rest.

One minute later, the telephone rang. He picked it up, knowing it would be Glenda calling him for an update. For the next ten minutes, he described what he had seen that morning and how the power at Sprite Towers was growing.

'The girls' power was very strong,' he told her. 'The house felt as if it might lift off!'

Then he told Glenda about what he had seen over Mum's head, as she opened the door to the tower. 'I'm sure they balance their magic by using the power of the four directions. The girls were standing against the walls of the tower. Flame was standing at the east side, opposite Ash on the west, and Marina was standing at the south side, opposite Ariel on the north.'

Glenda growled when she heard this and began to apply more pressure. 'The girls won't stop now, Charles,' she said. 'They're so close. You've *got* to go back tonight. They're sure to try again while you're not there.'

'But Glenda, I can't go creeping about Sprite Towers in the middle of the night!' he protested. 'It's one thing to be there in the daytime, but quite another to break into the house while everybody is asleep!"

'Charles, I *want* the secret of the towers,' Glenda said in her coolest, deadliest voice. 'Now go back there and get it for me – or there'll be no payment.'

The line went dead.

Charles stared across the room. Damn and blast, he thought. However am I going to get into the house? And what about that dratted dachshund? He may bark . . . Oh Lord, he thought. However did I get into this mess . . .

He looked at his watch. Eleven o'clock. Okay, I'll have three hours' sleep and then go back. If the girls do go up to the towers, they'll wait until their parents are asleep.

Then he set the alarm on his mobile phone, leaned back against the soft armchair and shut his eyes.

At two o'clock on Wednesday morning as Mum, Dad and Grandma slept soundly in their beds, the Sprite Sisters met in Flame's room. Despite the late hour, their faces were bright with excitement. Ariel was bouncing up and down.

'Shh,' whispered Flame. 'Calm down, Ariel! We don't want to get caught now. We're so close to finding the secret of the towers.'

Now, as the thin sliver of the new moon passed over the night sky, the Sprite Sisters climbed the stairs to the attics and opened the door to the West Tower.

At the same time, Charles Smythson parked his car at the bottom of the driveway and walked up to Sprite Towers.

As the girls closed the door of the West Tower and sat down in their four positions, Charles walked around to the back of the house.

How am I going to get in and without waking the dog, he wondered.

But he was in luck. Dad had got used to leaving the kitchen door unlocked while the girls had been camping, and that evening he'd forgotten they were sleeping in the house, not the caravan, so he'd left it unlocked. Charles turned the handle – and pushed open the door.

As Bert woke and was about to bark, Charles bent down and used his magic power to silence him. The little dog settled back down in his basket and went back to sleep, his memory of the intruder erased.

Charles opened the door to the back staircase and closed it behind him. Very carefully, he began to walk up the narrow, winding stairs. Under his left arm was his black notebook.

Upstairs, the West Tower was ablaze with light. All the colours of the rainbow pulsed through the room in waves – first red, then orange, then yellow, then green, then blue, indigo and violet. The four Sprite Sisters were still sitting in their four directions, their legs crossed, their backs against the wall. They gazed from side to side, amazed by the intensity of the light and the beautiful colours pulsating around them. They noticed that the noise of the wind in the trees, the sounds in the house – even the sound of their own breathing – receded. In the tower, everything was still silent.

As their power built, the colours of the spectrum merged into a band of bright white light, with the hues of the rainbow all around it. The light arced from the centre of the bare wooden floorboards, out through the wall towards the East Tower.

The Sprite Sisters got up from their positions and moved towards the west side of the room. In front of them, the shape of steps appeared in the arc of light and seemed to lead up and out of the tower, through the top of the wall. More steps appeared. On and on, up and up they went. The shape of the steps grew clearer and became denser, until they looked so solid the girls wondered if they could stand on them.

The Sprite Sisters gaped in awe.

'It's a bridge to the East Tower,' said Flame.

Ash stared at the bridge. In her hand, the magic stone squeaked loudly – and again. She felt it vibrating vigorously and saw that it was emitting a bright blue light.

'The stone!' said Ash. 'It's trying to tell us something!'

Flame and Marina heard her and saw the stone's blue light, but Ariel was transfixed. She heard and saw nothing but the bridge of light in front of her. She moved forward, a little ahead of her sisters, her face bright with anticipation.

'It *is* a portal!' she said, without turning.

'How do you know?' asked Flame, behind her.

'I can see it!' said Ariel, her eyes widening. 'It's not just going to the East Tower – it's a gateway in time. I can see it clear as day.'

She moved forward again, just a little, all the time looking up at the steps. She did not see the rainbow light touching her toes. She stepped forwards again, drawn by the light.

'Be careful!' shouted Ash, sensing Ariel had moved too close and reaching forward to grab her.

But it was too late.

In a flash, Ariel vanished.

For a few seconds, Flame, Marina and Ash were silent – unable to comprehend what had happened. They stood stunned, their hearts pounding, their throats dry with terror.

The next moment, all hell broke loose.

'*Ariel's gone!*' screamed Marina. '*She's disappeared!*'

The three Sprite Sisters stared in horror at the bridge of light.

'*Where is she? What's happened?*' shouted Ash, her face white with terror.

Flame gasped. 'I think she's passed through the portal!'

'*We must find her!*' cried Marina.

'But *how*?' shouted Flame.

'Should we follow her?' asked Ash, wide-eyed.

'She could be anywhere in time or space!' said Flame.

And in the next instant, Charles Smythson was standing

beside them, having crept into the tower room, unnoticed. Flame, Marina and Ash nearly fainted with surprise.

Charles stared at the bridge of light, his mouth open in astonishment, then he looked around at the girls – saw their terrified faces. They were crying, shouting at him, '*Do something! Do something!*'

'What's happened?' he shouted.

'Ariel's gone into the portal!' cried Flame, waving her arms at the rainbow of light. 'She's disappeared! We've got to find her!'

Charles stood stupefied. Was this the secret of the towers? A portal? A portal – to where?

He moved forward slightly, staring at the steps that rose up and away, through the wall towards the East Tower.

It's a bridge to the other tower, he thought, looking up at the steps. He could hear the girls crying, and wondered why no one else had come into the room, given the commotion, but he was so intrigued that everything, except the bridge of light, receded in his mind. The sounds around him grew faint. All he saw was the light.

He took a step forward and held out his hand. What does the light feel like, he wondered. It's so beautiful, he thought, smiling to himself. This beautiful, beautiful light with its white centre and its rainbow-coloured edges . . .

He raised his hand as if to touch it and took another step forward. The Sprite Sisters watched, holding their breath.

'Be careful!' shouted Flame. '*Charles, no!*'

But once again it was too late. Charles had come too

close to the portal – and he, too, vanished.

Flame, Marina and Ash screamed and clutched one another.

Ash felt the stone in her hand. It was vibrating again. She thought it was strange that Mum and Dad had not burst into the room. Surely they must have heard all the shouting, she thought, looking around at the door.

She gazed down again at the stone. What's happening, she wondered. The stone . . . the stone is trying to tell us something . . .

Ash gasped, her heart pumping hard. '*Wait!*' she shouted, putting out her hand. Flame and Marina spun around.

'What?' cried Flame. Beside her, Marina sobbed.

'*Wait!*' said Ash. 'Just wait . . . '

Then she said, 'Let's move back. Let's move back towards the wall.'

The three Sprite Sisters edged backwards.

'Just wait,' Ash repeated, softly but firmly. Flame and Marina gulped and breathed out heavily.

How long they stood there waiting, they had no idea. It felt like an eternity.

All the time, the three sisters stared up at the steps.

Then Flame looked high up to where the bridge of light passed through the wall. '*Oh!*' she cried, pointing. 'Look! *Look up there!*'

Marina and Ash gasped in amazement.

A figure was moving towards them, down the steps. In his arms was a small, slumped figure.

The Sprite Sisters stared, open-mouthed.

A young man – a tall young man with dark blond hair, wearing a soldier's uniform – was coming down the steps towards them, carrying Ariel. Behind him, Charles Smythson staggered down the steps.

Flame, Marina and Ash were speechless.

As he approached the bottom of the steps, the young man said nothing. In his arms, Ariel lay still, as if asleep.

'George!' whispered Flame. 'It's George Sprite!'

'George!' gasped Ash, staring at the man whose letter she had been carrying in her pocket.

'George!' squeaked Marina, unable to believe it.

George Sprite smiled at each of the three Sprite Sisters. They smiled back at him.

At the bottom of the bridge, he set Ariel down on her feet. She wobbled and he held her arm until she got her balance. She turned around to look up at him – and he smiled down at her. Then he gently pushed her forward, so that she was out of the arc of light.

As Ariel stepped on to the wooden floorboards of the West Tower, George stood to one side to allow Charles Smythson to step past him, then he turned and walked back up the steps and over the bridge of light.

Flame, Marina and Ash hugged their little sister, stroked her hair – and laughed with joy. She looked dizzy, as if all this was not quite real.

Charles Smythson stood on the wooden floorboards, crumpled and dazed. Then he moved to lean against the wall of the tower.

The rainbow light began to dim. When the Sprite Sisters looked again at the bridge of light, the figure of the young man had vanished.

'George has gone!' said Ash. 'And we didn't thank him!'

'Look! The bridge – it's fading!' said Marina, pointing.

The four Sprite Sisters watched as the light dimmed – and they were left standing in the dark. Suddenly, all the sounds in the house, the sound of their breathing, the wind in the trees were audible. As the magic disappeared, sound returned.

'Shh!' warned Flame, looking around her, conscious, suddenly, of where they were and what was happening. 'Be very quiet!'

She drew her little sister to her, and whispered, 'Thank heavens you're safe, Ariel!'

Ariel smiled woozily.

Standing in the dark, the four sisters hugged each other tight. As their eyes adjusted to the gloom, they looked around them.

'Where's Charles?' whispered Marina.

'He's gone – look the door's open!' whispered Flame.

Flame shivered. The thought that Charles Smythson had seen what they had seen, had learned what they had learned, disturbed her greatly. He knows our secret, she thought. He knows – everything . . .

Would he get out of the house without being found, she wondered. Would he tell their parents? And what would he tell Glenda Glass?

Suddenly, the cold of the room pierced the Sprite Sisters and with it the reality of where they were and what they were doing. Outside, they could hear the wind in the trees. They shivered and gasped.

'We must get back to bed – quick now!' Flame pushed Marina and Ariel towards the door.

'How come Mum and Dad didn't hear us?' whispered Marina.

'I don't know – we'll talk about it in the morning,' whispered Flame. 'Be very, very quiet, please,' she implored, leading Ariel down the rickety wooden stairs to the attics.

Ash started to follow her sisters, but the stone squeaked again. She stopped and stood, alone, in the tower room. A bright blue light began to glow from the stone on her outstretched hand, lighting up the room once more. Using it as a torch, Ash looked around the room.

There's something I have to find, she thought. I can feel it. Round the room she went, until she came back to the door.

And there it was, lying on the floor behind the door: Charles Smythson's black notebook.

Within ten minutes, the Sprite Sisters were sound asleep. Flame had taken Ariel to her room and tucked her up. Then she crept back along the corridor and got into her own bed. Marina fell into her bed like a stone.

Ash carried the magic stone and Charles's notebook back to her room. She put the stone under her pillow and the notebook under the bed. Then she climbed into bed and was asleep within seconds.

Charles Smythson staggered down the dark driveway of Sprite Towers. If anybody had seen him, they would have thought he was drunk from the way he wove from side to side.

After what felt like an age, he got back to his car. He opened the door, climbed in and slumped over the steering wheel. All he wanted to do was sleep. He felt exhausted, confused, disorientated.

Where have I been to, he wondered. What happened? That man who led me back – he looked familiar. Where have I seen that face?

Mustn't fall asleep here, he thought, rousing himself to consciousness. Must get back to The Oaks.

He turned on the interior light and checked his watch – nearly four o'clock – then struggled to get the key in the ignition.

How he got back to The Oaks, Charles never knew, when he thought about it later. He remembered driving, but not whether he turned on the headlights. He remembered opening the front door, but not whether he shut it behind him. And he remembered falling on to the bed.

When he woke seven hours later, fully clothed and lying on top of the bed, the memory of how he got there was a blur.

Oh no, he thought, seeing the clock beside the bed. He should have been at Sprite Towers hours ago. Quickly, he got up, had a shower and went downstairs. In the kitchen, the light was flashing on the answerphone.

Blast, he thought. It'll be Ottalie wondering where I've got to – and it was – along with a message from Glenda Glass, demanding that he call her the moment he got in.

I must get going, he thought, as he filled the kettle and switched it on. There's still a lot to finish off at Sprite Towers.

Fifteen minutes later, he began to feel alive again. Strong coffee and a good breakfast woke him up and his mind began to clear. He called Ottalie, apologised profusely, and told her he would be around shortly.

Then he gathered his things from the kitchen table. Mobile phone: he ignored the messages from Glenda and switched it off. Keys, yes got those. Notebook. Where's that gone?

He looked around. Where have I left it?

He scratched his head. When did I last see it, he thought, trying to work out where it might be. He ran up to his bedroom. Not there. He went out to the car – not there, either.

Then he stood in the hallway, a sense of mild panic creeping up on him.

Did I take it to Sprite Towers last night, he wondered, scratching his head.

Oh no, he thought. Don't say I left it in the tower . . . .

Drat, drat, drat, he realised. Yes, that's where it is.

Keep calm, he said to himself. There's no reason it won't still be there. It was dark. The girls would not have seen it. It will be there.

Locking the front door of The Oaks, he walked towards his car.

At Sprite Towers, the girls were still sleeping like logs.

'Whatever is the matter with them all?' Mum looked distracted. 'They never sleep this long!'

Grandma paced around the kitchen anxiously. She knew her granddaughters were safely in their beds, as she'd checked as soon as she had awoken. Nevertheless, she wanted to know what had happened last night.

To Mum, though, she said, 'I expect they're tired after their nights out camping. I doubt they got much sleep in the caravan. They just need to catch up. Don't worry, Ottalie – here, have a coffee.' And she handed Mum a cup.

'Where's Charles got to?' asked Mum, sitting down at the kitchen table. 'He rang to say he was on his way.'

'He must be tired as well,' said Grandma. 'He's been working very hard.'

'He has still got quite a few photographs to take,' said Mum. 'And I'd really like him to be finished by the time Anne and the family arrive on Friday.'

'He will be,' said Grandma. 'Everything will work out, you'll see.' But she still paced restlesly up and down the room.

CHAPTER THIRTEEN

THE BLACK NOTEBOOK

CHARLES SMYTHSON drove to Sprite Towers as quickly as he could.

I must get my notebook back, he thought, as he changed down a gear and roared around a bend on the narrow country road. Whatever was I thinking of taking it there last night? They must not find it. They must not...

He roared down the driveway of Sprite Towers and screeched to a halt at the front of the house.

Dad was opening the door as he got out of the car. 'Charles!' he called, cheerfully. 'How's it going? Nearly finished?'

'Morning, Colin,' he replied, through gritted teeth. The last thing he needed now was a hold up. The Sprite Sisters could be picking up his notebook this minute . . .

Dad looked hard at Charles. 'You okay, old chap? You look a bit peaky.'

'Bit of a rough night,' said Charles, smiling weakly.

'I expect you're anxious to get finished now,' said Dad. 'Nearly there.'

'Yes,' agreed Charles. 'Nearly there.'

'Well, it's been a pleasure to have you here,' said Dad. 'We've all enjoyed it and you've certainly brought a lot of interest and colour to the old house. I hope the work on the Sprite Towers inventory furthers your career.'

Charles looked into Dad's kind brown eyes and for a moment wondered how he could be behaving so badly to this man and his family. Colin Sprite was one of the nicest, most decent men he had ever met. And he, Charles, had deceived him, had tried to harm his daughters – had used his dark magic on one of them, and Colin's mother. He had broken into Colin's house in the middle of the night. He had tried to find out the family's secrets and – worst of all – he had relayed everything to Glenda Glass. How she would use the information, he could only guess, but it would likely be for her own, treacherous ends.

Charles looked at Dad again. As a Sprite, Colin was the exact opposite of Glenda Glass. She knew nothing of kindness or integrity. He lived it.

He saw the look of concern in Dad's eyes. Perhaps I should come clean and tell him, he thought. Perhaps I should tell him about the power in this house. Perhaps I should tell him how gifted his daughters are. Perhaps I should warn him about Glenda . . .

He wanted to speak – to confess, to apologise – but the words felt as if they were stuck in his throat.

He was looking at Dad, but it was Glenda Glass's voice that began to ring in the back of his mind.

'Thank you, Colin,' he said, looking down at the ground, unable to meet his gaze.

Dad waited. Then he said, 'Okay, well if you're sure everything is all right.'

'Yes, yes,' said Charles, summoning all his strength and smiling his dazzling smile once more. 'Everything is fine.'

'See you later then – I'm going to the office in town for a meeting,' said Dad, and he walked off to his car.

Charles stepped in through the front door. His first instinct was to run up the stairs to the tower, but he knew Ottalie would be waiting for him. Resisting the temptation, he walked through the hallway to the kitchen.

'Morning,' he said, as he came through the door.

'Morning, Charles!' said Mum, brightly. 'Coffee?'

'Yes, please,' he said.

'Sit down,' said Mum, and she got up to pour him a cup.

'Morning, Marilyn,' he said to Grandma, as he sat down at the kitchen table.

'Morning, Charles,' she replied, looking at him steadily. 'You look as if you haven't slept much.'

Charles smiled. 'That's what Colin said. Bit of a rough night, I'm afraid.'

'Oh?' said Grandma, raising an eyebrow.

Before he could answer, Mum handed him a cup of coffee.

'Thanks, Ottalie,' he said. He looked around the kitchen. 'It's very quiet here today. Where are the girls?'

'Still asleep!' said Mum, pushing her blond hair back from her pretty face.

'Oh?' replied Charles, sipping his coffee quickly.

'Yes, I was going to wake them, but Marilyn thinks they need their rest.' Mum smiled at her mother-in-law.

'Kids, eh?' said Charles.

'Hmm,' agreed Mum. 'So, Charles – are you nearly there?'

'Yes, yes,' he said. 'I'll be out of your hair before the family arrives, don't worry.'

'What will you be doing today?' asked Mum.

'The photography on the third floor and the top of the staircase,' said Charles. 'I need to get going.'

'And when you've left here, you're off to the National Portrait Gallery, to piece all the research together?' said Mum.

'Yes, there and the Witt Library Archives at the Courtauld Institute,' said Charles, finishing his coffee. 'I'll compare the photographs I've taken and notes I've made here against other portraits in the archives. It's a process of filtering and refining the information. There might be other portraits by the same painters, or portraits of the same sitters by different painters. I piece it all together, then write the inventory.'

'How many portraits have we got at Sprite Towers altogether, Charles?' asked Mum.

'Forty-six, that I've documented,' he replied. 'And within that number, you've a good mix of full – that is, whole length – as well as half-portraits, the head and shoulder paintings.'

Mum smiled at Grandma. 'Forty-six portraits, eh!'

'It's a good number,' smiled Grandma.

'So, when will we get the finished inventory?' asked Mum.

'It depends on how the research goes, but I should expect to get it completed within a few weeks,' said Charles, looking around anxiously.

'Super!' said Mum. 'We look forward to seeing it.'

Charles stood up. 'Well, I'll press on, if that's okay – and thank you for the coffee.'

'You're very welcome,' said Mum.

Charles Smythson ran up the wide mahogany staircase. Up and up he went, right to the attics corridor. Then he stopped, waited and listened. All was still.

The girls must still be asleep, he thought. He turned to open the small wooden door that led up to the West Tower, then mounted the rickety steps. At the top, he opened the door to the tower and walked into the room.

He spun around. Where is it, he thought. *Where is it?*

The tower room was empty. No black notebook lying on the floor.

Damn and blast! He stood, cursing, for a moment.

Now what, he wondered. Where can it be?

He thought back on his night-time visit. Yes, I remember

– I had it under my left arm, as I walked up the back staircase. So where is it now?

The Sprite Sisters: they must have it, he thought. Oh no . . . oh no . . .

Charles sighed heavily. He walked over to the side of the tower room and leaned back against the wall.

Did that really happen, he wondered, looking around the room. Was there really a bridge with steps, which came down in the middle of this floor? Did I really walk through the portal? Who was it that led me back here?

It was all so strange, he thought.

The room still felt alive with power, he thought, looking up. That was an *amazing* experience. I wonder what Ariel saw?

At about the same time that morning, Flame, Marina and Ash were sitting on Ariel's bed.

'So tell us! Tell us what you saw!' they said.

The little blonde sister took a deep breath.

'Come on, Ariel – tell us what happened!' said Flame.

'Well,' she said. 'It's like this . . .'

They waited.

'Like what?' said Marina.

Ariel giggled.

'What *happened* as you stepped into the light?' asked Flame, getting impatient.

Ariel's brow furrowed with concentration. She chewed her lip and put her hand under her chin. 'Well, it was really weird . . . I remember walking up the bridge of light . . .'

'We didn't see you do that – you just vanished,' said Flame.

'Did I?'

'Yes. One moment you were with us in the room and the next you'd gone,' said Flame. 'We were *terrified*!'

Ariel nodded, still staring into space.

'So what happened?' probed Flame.

'George was there!' Ariel smiled and looked around at her sisters.

'Where?'

'Standing there in front of me,' said Ariel. 'On the bridge.'

'What did he say?' asked Flame.

'Say? Oh, he didn't say anything!'

'How did you know it was George?'

'Because he looked just like the young man in the portrait of course, silly!'

'So what was around you, when you met him?'

Ariel sunk her face on her hands and screwed up her mouth. 'Hmm,' she said. 'Well – light. You know, like the rainbow-edged light you saw.'

'Was there anything behind him?' asked Flame. 'A building or a room?'

'There was . . . there was a garden,' she said, staring ahead of her, trying to see the image in her mind.

'A garden?' asked Marina. 'Our garden?'

'I don't know,' said Ariel, biting her lip. 'There was an arch – like a church or a ruin. And roses – rambling roses all over the ruin . . .'

She was silent for a second, then said, wistfully, 'I *smelled* roses. It was lovely.'

Flame, Marina and Ash sat open-mouthed.

'Did you see anyone else?' asked Flame.

Ariel started. 'Only Charles.' She frowned. 'I was frightened when I saw him. I thought he was coming after me.'

'Is that why you fainted?' asked Flame.

'Faint? Did I faint?'

'Well, George was carrying you in his arms,' said Flame.

'S'pose I must've done then,' agreed Ariel, pursing her lips. 'I don't usually faint.'

'No, but you don't usually go through portals!' Flame laughed.

'True,' giggled Ariel.

'What did Charles do while you were in the portal?' asked Ash. 'Did he speak to George? Did he get any information from him?'

'I don't remember,' replied Ariel. 'I just remember seeing George and smelling the roses, then seeing Charles behind me – then George setting me on my feet and seeing you standing the other side of the light.' She turned to look at her sisters. 'Why – what did Charles do?'

'I don't know,' said Flame. 'He came down the steps after you and George.'

'He looked very dazed and confused,' added Ash.

'I think you were both only gone for a minute, but it felt like an age to us – we were so worried,' said Flame.

'Why was Charles here, in the tower?' asked Ariel. 'How did he know we were going to use our power at that time of night?'

'Good question,' said Flame. 'He must have worked out that we'd want to try while we were alone – and that would have to be at night.'

'It was spooky the way he was there, suddenly, standing beside us,' said Marina. She shivered. 'He gives me the creeps. It's like having Glenda close by.'

Flame looked thoughtful. 'Grandma always says things do not happen by chance: that everything is connected. If that is the case, why did Charles go through the portal and not us?'

'Because he shares the same curious, reckless traits that Ariel does, of course!' retorted Marina.

'Yes, but what does it mean?' asked Ash.

'It means he shares our secret – and that Glenda Glass will too, if he hasn't already told her,' said Flame, glumly.

'If Grandma is right, there is a reason why he is meant to share it,' said Marina. 'I don't understand. It just puts us at more risk . . .'

'We don't know what it means at the moment, but I'm sure we'll understand soon,' said Flame. 'Anyway, we know Glenda Glass is not going to leave us alone. That's been obvious since she moved to The Oaks. We thought we'd be free of her this summer, but she's still hounding us through her spy, Charles.'

Ariel screwed up her nose. 'I'd like to ask Charles what he saw,' she said.

Flame drew a sharp breath. 'I'm not sure that's wise, Ariel. I think you should stay quiet.'

'But he may ask me,' said Ariel.

'You don't have to answer,' cautioned Flame. 'Somehow, though, we have to turn this to our advantage and get information from Charles without giving anything away.'

'The other really weird thing is why Mum and Dad didn't come in,' said Marina. 'We were shouting and yelling – and they must have heard!'

'Did you notice how all the sounds outside receded, when the light came?' said Flame.

'Yes,' her sisters agreed.

Flame continued. 'It was almost as if we were in a bubble. Maybe no sound came out of the room – so Mum and Dad wouldn't have heard anything. Maybe only we were hearing the racket, as we were in the "bubble".'

Ash sat up with a start. 'I've just remembered something!' she said. She jumped off Ariel's bed, opened the door and ran down the corridor to her own room. There, she leaned under her bed and pulled out Charles Smythson's black notebook. With this in her hand, she ran back to Ariel's room.

'Look!' she said.

'What is it?' asked Ariel.

'It's Charles's notebook,' said Ash. 'He left it in the tower room last night.'

She handed it to Flame, who opened it on her lap. Marina, Ash and Ariel moved closer around her. Flame began to flip through the pages, stopping every now and then.

'Oh, my golly gosh!' she said, staring at a page covered with Charles's handwriting.

'What?' asked Ash.

'This is just what we need!' said Flame. 'We've something to bargain with here. I should think Charles is in a complete panic, knowing he's left this in the tower room – and that we have probably found it. It has got all his research in it.'

She was right. As the Sprite Sisters sat on Ariel's bed looking at the notebook, Charles was racing up the wide mahogany staircase to the tower room. Ash had missed bumping into him on the corridor by seconds only.

Marina, Ash and Ariel waited as Flame scoured the notebook. All the time she made comments. 'Notes about the pictures . . . more notes about pictures . . .'

Then she stopped. 'Hey, look at this,' she said.

Marina, Ash and Ariel stared. There, on the page, were the initials, *GG* followed by a long number.

'It's a French phone number,' said Flame. '00 33 is the French country code. *GG* must be Glenda Glass – and we know she's in France. It just proves that Charles was lying when he said he didn't know her.'

'Shall we ring the number?' suggested Ash.

'What would we say?' said Flame, quickly. 'No, it may better that Glenda doesn't know that we know. We can let Charles know we know, though – and we must make a note of that number.'

Marina sneered. 'Horrible woman is probably out there spending the money she stole from Grandma.'

Flame continued to read through the notebook. 'Charles has written about the feeling of light and energy in the house. Listen: *The power is building. The girls came into the house early this morning and worked on the third floor. By the time I arrived, the house was full of a strong blue light.*'

Flame flipped to the latest set of notes and pointed. 'And here he's drawn the crossed circle with the lines going through each of the four directions. Look – he's marked in our positions, and he's got them right. See those little circles at each of the four directions and the letters *F*, *M*, *As* and *Ar*. He must know where we stand to build the magic power in the house – and that the sign of the crossed circle represents this.'

Flame's eyes narrowed. She looked anxiously at her sisters. 'This is worrying.'

'Why?' asked Marina, frowning.

'It means Charles knows how we work together – that he understands the dynamic of our magic power,' said Flame. 'He will know that we work as a team and that our strength is in the balance of our power. He will be able to deduce that I have the power of Fire, that Marina's power is Water, Ash's is Earth and that Ariel works with Air.'

'But surely Glenda would have worked that out – when we were at the concert,' said Marina.

Flame nodded. 'Maybe – but now Charles can confirm it. The more he knows about our magic, the easier it will be to turn it back on us.'

'But we do have his notebook,' reminded Marina.

Flame grinned. 'Yes, we do have that.'

'Do you think the sign of the crossed circle in the house is meant for us?' asked Ash, suddenly. 'Or have there been four other Sprites before us, who worked together as we do?'

'I don't know, Ash,' replied Flame. She looked thoughtful, then returned to the notebook. She flipped back a page and peered at Charles's handwriting. 'Hey, this is interesting: *Higgens – £5000 by 25th – 993 4517. Stanford – £3500 by 26th – 331 9021.* Who are Higgens and Stanford, I wonder?' She stared at the page, deep in concentration, then said, 'Payments he has to make, maybe – and soon, by the looks of it. It's the fifteenth today.'

As the Sprite Sisters considered this, Marina looked around at the door and said suddenly, 'Quick! Mum's outside talking to Charles!'

They all jumped off the bed. Flame grabbed the black notebook and held it behind her back as Mum came into the room.

'Oh, you're up at last!' she said. 'I was beginning to wonder what had happened to you!'

'Hi, Mum,' they all said. Ariel, Ash and Marina gave her a hug. Flame held back.

'Now, go and have a shower, all of you,' she said. 'Then come on down – it's nearly lunchtime.'

Grandma had followed Mum up the stairs and now appeared in the bedroom doorway. She caught Flame's eye.

Behind her, in the corridor, Charles Smythson was hovering, his face taut with anxiety.

As Mum came out of the room, she said, 'Charles, the

girls are getting dressed. Please would you pop downstairs for ten minutes?'

'Yes, of course, Ottalie.' He smiled his dazzling smile, then turned and caught Flame's eye through the open doorway. Her face coloured, as she stood holding the notebook behind her back.

She's got it, he thought. Flame's got my blasted notebook! Then he turned and stomped downstairs.

As soon as Mum's back was turned, Flame handed the notebook to Grandma. 'Please guard this – it's going to be useful,' she whispered, urgently. 'And don't look Charles in the eye – he's after it.'

Grandma looked quizzically at the notebook. 'I'll look at it closely, dear.'

Downstairs the phone rang. Charles answered it and called up the stairs, 'Ottalie – phone for you!'

'Coming!' she shouted back and left the room.

Ash shut the bedroom door. The Sprite Sisters crowded around, as Grandma sat down on the end of Ariel's bed and opened up the black notebook. 'Go on, shoo – all of you!' she said. 'Go and get showered and dressed before your mother comes back. Shut the door again and let me read this in peace.'

For the next ten minutes, Marilyn Sprite read the notebook. She learned a lot and made some perceptive decisions about Charles Smythson.

When the girls were dressed and the beds made, she and the Sprite Sisters came down the wide mahogany staircase. Grandma carried the notebook in her left hand

and held it close to her body. Charles waited at the bottom, his face tense and determined, his eyes focused on the notebook.

From the drawing room, Mum's voice could be heard talking on the telephone.

'I'd like my notebook back, Marilyn,' said Charles, looking her in the eye and holding out his hand. This time, she met his gaze.

'All in good time, Charles,' she replied. 'I think we need to have a little chat first.'

After lunch, Mum went out to do some food shopping and asked Marina and Ariel to go with her.

The black notebook was safe and Dad was still at the office as Grandma, Flame, Ash and Charles Smythson went out to the terrace and sat down around the large wooden table.

Charles sat down at the end and leaned back in his chair. He crossed his arms over his chest. He was already seething – none of them had brought the notebook.

Grandma sat down, along the long side of the table, on Charles's right side. Flame and Ash sat opposite her.

Grandma leaned forward on the table and looked directly at Charles. 'I'd like a straight talk with no silly tricks, please,' she said.

Charles raised an eyebrow. 'Tricks?'

'No magic power, please, Charles. No wiping of memory. Let's negotiate.'

'Why?'

'Because I have your notebook and you want it back,' she said, flashing the briefest of smiles.

'Where is it?' he asked, sharply.

'Marina has it in the little rucksack she carries when she goes out,' said Grandma. 'It is packed up, stamped and ready to post. Providing I text her within the next twenty-five minutes, she will *not* put it into the postbox at the supermarket, where they're currently shopping.'

Charles gulped. 'And who is it addressed to?'

'Stephen Glass,' said Grandma, crisply.

Charles half-smiled, half-snarled, unfolded his arms and sat up in his chair. For a few seconds he was silent. Then he growled, 'Okay. Let's get on with it.'

He glared menacingly at Grandma. She sat straight and alert, and looked him in the eye. Then she spoke crisply. 'Charles, you have the magic power that runs through the Sprite family. Unfortunately, you have chosen to use it unwisely and unkindly. You have hurt my family and have chosen to inflict further damage through your connection with Glenda Glass. You have taken something from us – and now we have taken something from you. We are happy to return your notebook on the proviso that you answer some questions.'

'Such as?'

'Such as, how well do you know Glenda Glass?'

Charles breathed out heavily and stared at the ground, silent.

'Such as, is Glenda Glass paying you money for the information you have and will give her about the girls' powers?' said Grandma.

Charles rubbed his hand across his mouth and moved uneasily in his seat, but stared at the ground.

Grandma turned to Flame. 'How long have we got before Marina posts the notebook?' she asked.

Flame looked at her watch. 'Twenty minutes,' she said.

Charles glanced at her, then looked back at Grandma.

'You have less than twenty minutes, Charles,' said Grandma. She waited for a few seconds, then said, 'Does Glenda pay you?'

Charles crossed, uncrossed and crossed his arms and turned away from her. 'Yes,' he replied angrily. 'Yes, she pays me money.'

'Do you have gambling debts?' asked Grandma.

Charles looked around at her, astonished. 'What? What! How do you know that?'

Grandma raised her left eyebrow. 'The information in your notebook suggested debts owing, which you have just confirmed. I made an intuitive guess about the gambling. Well, *do* you gamble?'

'Yes,' Charles replied.

'And do you have gambling debts?'

'Yes . . .' His voice trailed off and he moved uncomfortably in his seat.

'I rather think you need the names and phone numbers written in the notebook,' said Grandma.

Charles was silent, his face reddened.

'Does Glenda know about this?' asked Grandma.

Charles looked at her sharply. 'Yes, she knows.'

'And is the money she will pay you for this "assignment" enough to clear your current debts?' asked Grandma.

Charles sank, slightly, in his seat and stared, once more, at the ground. For a moment he was silent. Then he said, quietly, 'Yes.'

'So you will soon have reached a point where you could be free of Glenda – if you chose to be – and live independently?'

Charles looked her, pensively. 'Yes, I suppose so,' he agreed.

'*If* you are strong enough,' said Grandma.

'Yes,' he agreed. 'If I am strong enough.'

'Well, I leave that up to you, Charles. It's your decision as to how you lead your life.'

Charles's face was thoughtful and he rubbed his chin with his hand.

Then Grandma changed tack. 'How many husbands has Glenda had, Charles?'

He looked at her, surprised. 'Er, four, I think,' he replied. 'Why?'

'And what happened to them?'

Charles hesitated.

'Did any of them, for instance, die?' asked Grandma.

Charles drew breath.

'Seventeen minutes left,' said Flame, looking at her watch.

'Did any of Glenda's husbands die, Charles?'

'Yes,' he replied.

'All of them?' asked Grandma.

Charles looked around at her and caught her gaze, utterly perplexed. Grandma waited, her green eyes focused and determined. Charles shrugged and said, 'Yes, I think so. I don't know for sure – nobody does – but I have a hunch.'

'Do you know the name of her last husband?'

'I think it might have been Pierre,' replied Charles – noticing that Marilyn Sprite flinched, very slightly, at this name.

'How do you know?'

Charles shrugged again. 'Sometimes, Glenda likes to talk. I've heard her mention the name Pierre.'

'Did you meet Pierre?'

'Good Lord, no!' replied Charles. 'I rarely see Glenda and I've never met any of her husbands.'

'Does your father have any contact with her?' asked Grandma.

Charles shook his head. 'Not as far as I know,' he said.

'Where do you think Glenda's money comes from?'

Charles unfolded his arms, sat up and looked at Grandma. 'I assume it is from her husbands,' he said, quietly – and noted the tension that passed, fleetingly, over Marilyn Sprite's face.

'Are you aware that her last husband, Pierre, was my late husband's lawyer?' she asked.

Charles's eyes widened. 'No!' Again he saw the look of tension in her face – noticed Flame and Ash look at her. 'Why, what's happened? What's this about?'

Marilyn eyed him, silent and wary. Then she spoke, in a very deliberate voice. 'When my husband, Sheldon, died in the south of France five years ago, his lawyer ran off with my inheritance. I have reason to believe that Glenda was married to the lawyer and might have been behind the theft. The lawyer himself died in mysterious circumstances only a few days later. Unfortunately, by that time, the money had been taken from our account. It has never been found, despite an extensive police investigation.'

Charles looked astonished. 'What!'

Grandma watched him, like a hawk.

'Glenda *robbed* you?' said Charles. His face spoke of genuine amazement

Grandma smoothed her strawberry-blond bob and said crisply, 'I believe so. You may well be surprised. One Sprite robbing another Sprite.'

They were all silent. Flame looked at her watch again. 'Twelve minutes left,' she said. Charles tensed in his seat and rubbed his hand across his face.

'What are you going to tell Glenda about your experience last night?' asked Grandma.

Charles opened both his hands wide. 'What can I say?' he implored. 'She'll expect me to tell her everything!'

'*Which is?*' Grandma looked as if her patience was beginning to wear thin and Charles sensed it.

'Which is – that there is a portal that can be accessed in the West Tower, by the Sprite Sisters sitting in their places of the four directions.'

Grandma looked him in the eye. 'And where does the portal lead?'

Charles shrugged. 'Well, I think it may be back into

Sprite family history . . . I mean – we met George Sprite. He led us out again.'

'Why does Glenda want this power?' asked Grandma.

'Perhaps she thinks it will enable her to control the Sprite family's destiny,' said Charles. 'Who knows? I do know that she is desperate to own Sprite Towers and that she believes Sidney Sprite should never have been given the secret plan. She believes her great-grandmother, Lily, should have given it to Margaret, Glenda's own grand-mother.'

Grandma smiled. 'And do you agree?'

'Me?' Charles shrugged again. 'I have no idea. It doesn't bother me either way.'

'Ten minutes to go,' said Flame, looking at her watch.

Charles glanced at Flame, then looked at Grandma, his eyes suddenly beseeching.

'Listen, Marilyn, I may be bad, but I'm not all bad,' he said. 'I want, more than anything, to progress in my career as an art historian – but I've a weakness with gambling and I've got caught up with Glenda Glass. So far, I've found it hard to get out of this mess.'

'Don't forget you like money,' reminded Grandma. 'You are a man with expensive tastes.'

'Yes,' he sighed. 'I like money.'

'And what part does Stephen Glass play in this?' asked Grandma. 'Is he aware of his mother's magic power and her evil ways?'

Charles shook his head. 'No, I don't think so. Stephen is a good chap. As far as I can tell, he doesn't have the

Sprite magic power – and I think he'd be appalled if he knew a quarter of what his mother had done.' He sighed. 'Stephen would be very upset to think I'd hurt you all in any way. He's fond of the family – and apparently so is his daughter, Verena.'

For a moment, Charles looked genuinely sorry.

'Eight minutes,' said Flame.

'How does Glenda feel about her son?' asked Grandma.

'It's interesting,' said Charles, shuffling in his seat, then looking up at her. 'I have wondered if Stephen is Glenda's weak spot – the one chink in her armour. I think he may be the only person she has ever loved.'

Grandma smiled, ironically, then said. 'Yet she abandoned him – didn't see him for years and years.'

'Yes,' agreed Charles.

'Are you frightened of Glenda?' asked Grandma, looking him in the eye.

He nodded. 'Yes. She's obsessed – for instance about Sprite Towers. She stops at nothing. She's a very scary woman. And, it's like . . . it's as if she sees through everything. You can't fool her . . .'

'Five minutes,' Flame broke in.

Charles sat up sharply. 'Please, Marilyn!' he said.

She looked at him coldly. 'Okay, Charles, you can have your notebook back. However, I have taken a photocopy of the contents. If I learn that you have caused us harm in any way in the future, I shall hand the copies to Stephen Glass. Since he is so influential in your career, this will be a big blow to you. I also have the phone numbers of the people you owe money – and I have Glenda's number. She might be a bit surprised to learn how I came across it.'

Charles gulped. 'I understand.'

'I believe you when you say she sees through you,' said Grandma. 'But if you *ever* try to hurt my grand-daughters again, I swear I shall come after you like there is no tomorrow.'

Charles's brown eyes clouded for a second. 'I under-stand,' he repeated, bowing his head.

'I'm not letting you off the hook entirely,' said Grandma. 'I may need information from you myself in the months to come. That is the price you pay for getting tangled up in a web of deceit. I strongly recommend that you get out of it and pursue your life and career openly and honestly.'

'Three minutes,' said Flame. Charles looked around at her anxiously.

'Marilyn!' he implored.

'Okay,' she agreed. She looked at Ash. 'Please text your sister and ask her to text back, to confirm she has got the message.'

Charles breathed out heavily and sat forward, his head in his hands, as Ash punched out the text message to Marina.

Grandma watched him, then said, 'In many ways, Charles, you are a super chap. You have everything – intelligence, good looks, charm, talent. Don't waste it all. Find your strength and have integrity in your life. At the moment, you're heading up a one-way street. We're all faced with choices in life. The trick is to make the right choice.'

The sound of Dad's car on the drive surprised them. 'Dad's home,' said Ash, looking around.

Flame and Ash stood up and headed to the front of the house to greet their father at the front door. Grandma and Charles got up and walked to the kitchen door.

As Grandma opened the door, she turned and said, 'Don't let Glenda run – and ruin – your life. You're worth more than that.'

He nodded, his eyes sad. 'Thank you, Marilyn,' he said. For the second time that day, he felt like a heel and a cheat.

'Will you tell Glenda about this conversation?' asked Grandma.

Charles pushed out his lips and stared ahead. 'I don't know,' he said.

'Well, if I were you I'd keep it to yourself,' advised Grandma.

Charles nodded. 'Yes, you're right,' he said. Then he said, 'Will you tell Colin and Ottalie?'

'Not if you keep your side of the bargain.' Then she said, gently, 'Do you feel comfortable hurting us like this?'

'No,' said Charles, shaking his head. 'But I don't have any choice.'

'One *always* has a choice, Charles,' said Grandma. Her green eyes glittered. 'Sort yourself out and blaze through this promising career. That's what I'd do.'

Charles bit his lip and nodded.

'Right,' said Grandma. 'Let's press on, shall we?'

CHAPTER FOURTEEN

CRICKET AT SPRITE TOWERS

ON FRIDAY morning, after days of gloomy weather, the clouds dispersed and the sun shone brightly. Everybody at Sprite Towers was flying around. Anne and Geoff and their three children would arrive after lunch.

As always, Mum, Dad and Grandma had been well organised. On Thursday it had been all hands on deck as the house was cleaned from top to bottom, the bedrooms were prepared and food and wine bought. Meanwhile, Charles had worked quietly to complete his inventory.

But there was always more to do at Sprite Towers: now there were vegetables and fruit to be picked from the garden, meals to be prepared and cakes to be baked for the cricket match the next day. Mum insisted that the Sprite

Sisters clean out the caravan and air their sleeping bags in the sunshine. Flame and Ash built a new campfire in readiness for the evening, when the whole family would gather around it.

Most important of all, to Dad at least, was the cricket field. He was up at the crack of dawn to mow the grass and mark out the oval boundary on the wide lawn. In the middle of this was a carefully-measured and marked out wicket and crease.

The match would begin at ten o'clock. There would be breaks for lunch at one o'clock and tea at four o'clock. The teams would play until they were all out. After the match finished – hopefully before seven o'clock – the Sprites planned a barbecue party. Although they lived abroad, Anne and Geoff travelled a lot and kept up with their British friends. Some of these friends had been invited to play in the match and others to the party.

For all the Sprites, Saturday would be a long and busy day.

Meanwhile, Charles Smythson was still moving lights, cable and photographic umbrellas along the corridors and working as quickly as he could to complete the photography. Alas, he had not achieved this on Thursday, as he had planned. Now, he apologised profusely as everybody raced past, but he need not have worried. Mum and Dad took it in their stride.

'Don't worry, Charles!' said Dad, as he clambered past. 'I have four daughters and I'm quite used to everything being topsy-turvy at Sprite Towers!'

Then he turned around and said, 'You are going to stay for cricket and the party tomorrow, aren't you?'

'Er – well, I was planning to go back to London,' said Charles.

'Nonsense!' said Dad. 'You can't miss a Sprite Towers cricket match! It's the best fun in all the world! It'll be a fabulous day! You must stay – I insist!'

Charles was non-plussed. He was anxious to get away as soon as possible. Then Dad said, 'You're a batsman, aren't you? I remember we talked about it last week.'

Charles smiled. 'Yes,' he replied. 'I played for my university.'

'Fantastic!' said Dad. He walked off, shouting, 'You *have* to stay, Charles! We need you!'

Charles slumped. Never, in his life, had he been made to feel more welcome than he had been by Colin and Ottalie Sprite – and yet he had betrayed them. The happier the family seemed, the more miserable he felt. He was relieved that, since handing back the notebook, the girls had hardly spoken to him.

He had returned to The Oaks on the Wednesday evening prepared for a telephone grilling from Glenda Glass – and he got it. However, the conversation was even more traumatic than he had expected.

She wanted to know everything.

What happened in the portal? How did the girls react? What did he see around George? What did he think it all meant? What happened to the light?

On and on went Glenda's questions, until Charles was

216

exhausted. Finally, he managed to get her off the phone. Then he climbed into bed, the black notebook beside him on the little table – Marina had handed it back to him on her return from the supermarket – and fell into a deep sleep.

When the Aussies arrived at Sprite Towers, there was great excitement. Outside the front of the house, everybody was shouting and hugging each other. The men shook hands and slapped each other on the back. The cousins kissed, awkwardly. The women kissed everyone. Mum and Anne cried. The grown-ups told the children they'd grown.

Anne and Geoff looked well and happy. Jamie – who was fifteen, loved surfing, had curly sun-bleached hair and a wide smile – and had grown even taller. Then there was Lottie, who was fourteen and wore braces. She had chestnut-brown hair, warm brown eyes and square shoulders.

'Hey, what pretty girls! You two look so alike!' Mum said to Lottie and Ash, as they stood together.

'They're just like Anne and Colin!' said Grandma, looking proudly at her family.

Then there was Daniel, who was twelve. A broad-shouldered boy with sandy hair, he stood with his hands in his pockets and kicked bits of gravel around the drive. He looked like his father, Geoff, and had a laugh to match.

As Charles Smythson tried to finish off his work inside the house, the rest of the Sprite family sat on the terrace. There was much to catch up on and the conversation bowled along.

The Sprite Sisters and their cousins ran down to the caravan and opened cold cans of fizzy drinks.

'Cool,' said Jamie, bending his long body through the door of the caravan.

Daniel climbed in after him, opened all the cupboard doors. 'Neat,' he said.

'Wow!' said Lottie, standing outside and looking around. 'You're so lucky to have this camp!'

'Yeah, we've had great fun,' said Flame.

Daniel appeared in the caravan doorway. 'Can we all camp out here?' he asked.

Flame smiled. 'Yes, we're going to put up some tents – but Mum says not tonight. She says we have to wait till after the match tomorrow – but we will have a campfire this evening.'

'Awesome,' said Daniel.

Back on the terrace, Dad and Geoff were finalising their teams. Geoff had asked some of his Aussie friends who lived in the UK to play, and they were bringing their families and staying locally. Jamie, Daniel and Lottie would play on his team.

Dad had invited some of his friends and their sons – including the Drysdale's boys, Vivek and Quinn – to play for his team. Flame and Marina would play for the home team as they could throw well. Batty Blenkinsop would be umpire.

The match had begun to take on Herculean proportions. Mum, Anne and Grandma listened to the men, much amused. 'How come our husbands become like gladiators when they play cricket?' Anne asked Mum. Grandma laughed.

After this, the Sprites played tennis, croquet on the lawn at the left hand side of the drive and the French game boules, on the gravel in the Secret Garden. Daniel, Ash and Ariel raced bicycles through the trees and down the driveway.

In the late afternoon, Charles Smythson finished the photography at Sprite Towers and packed up his equipment. Mum and Dad followed him out to his car.

'All done at last then,' said Dad. 'Thank you so much for all your efforts, Charles. It's much appreciated.'

'Thank you both for having me here,' said Charles, shaking Colin's hand, then kissing Ottalie on the cheek.

'See you tomorrow!' said Dad. 'We'll trounce the Aussies!'

After supper, as the new moon rose high in the sky, the Sprite family sat around the campfire down beside the Wild Woods.

Jamie played his guitar and Flame her fiddle. Ash, Marina and Lottie performed percussion on a variety of saucepans and tin cans, while Ariel played her flute and Daniel played Ariel's harmonica. Everyone else clapped.

They all joined in the choruses as Geoff sang 'Waltzing Matilda' in a loud voice, followed by 'Tie Me Kangaroo Down'. Everyone laughed.

Then Dad sang the 'Banana Boat Song', to which everyone chorused *'Daylight come and I want to go home'* every other line.

Mum and Anne sang 'She'll Be Coming Around The Mountain', with great gusto. By the time they'd all sung 'Clementine', 'Green Grow the Rushes', 'Danny Boy', 'Skip To My Lou', 'Drunken Sailor' and 'Streets of London', everyone was ready for bed. At which point, Dad and Geoff sang, 'Show Me The Way To Go Home'.

The Sprite Sisters damped down the campfire and shut the door of the caravan.

'Early start tomorrow,' said Mum, as they all walked back over the lawn.

'It's lovely to be here,' said Anne, beside her.

Mum put her arm around Anne's shoulders. 'It's wonderful to have you here,' she smiled. 'We miss you all, being so far away.'

'Yes,' agreed Anne. 'Sydney's a fantastic place to live, but it's always good to come back to Sprite Towers.'

Saturday morning broke warm and sunny.

'Thank heavens,' said Dad, looking up at the sky.

'And we've some breeze, too,' said Geoff. 'That'll help to keep us cool.'

The family sat down to breakfast on the terrace. Dad, Geoff, Jamie and Daniel wore their cricket whites. Flame, Lottie and Marina wore white T-shirts and shorts and put their hair in ponytails. Mum, Grandma, Anne and the other ladies and girls – including Ash and Ariel – wore pretty summer dresses.

Mum took photos of the teams and the spectators. 'This is wonderful!' she laughed.

Batty Blenkinsop was the first person to arrive. He carried his white umpire's coat and a Panama hat. After a quick cup of coffee, he walked round the cricket field and inspected the pitch with Dad and Geoff.

'Grass is looking very trim, Colin,' he said. 'I can see you've been busy.'

In the kitchen, the rest of the family worked hard. Several ladies from the village arrived to help with the food: there was a lot to do with lunch, tea and the barbecue supper to prepare.

Tables and chairs were carried down to the side of the cricket field. Colourful cloths were spread over the tables. Trays of glasses were laid out, followed by huge jugs of iced homemade lemonade and elderflower cordial.

Soon, the players and their families began to arrive. At ten o'clock sharp, Batty Blenkinsop tossed the coin. Geoff's team won and the Aussies went in to bat. The opening batsman, Scottie, scored a half-century and the match got off to a roaring start. Geoff, the second batsman scored thirty runs.

Everyone played their best. The English team ran and jumped and dived for the ball. The Aussies batted hard. The audience clapped and shouted.

By lunchtime, the Aussies had 118 runs and four men out. Despite this resounding start, the English team came in to their own after lunch. The combination of Quinn's bowling, Vivek's fielding skills and Dad's enthusiasm finally had the Australian team all out at two-thirty p.m. with a score of 159 runs.

There was a quick changeover of sides. The Australian team took up their fielding positions and the English batsmen put on their pads.

The Australians unleashed their fast bowler as Charles Smythson came in to bat at number three. He played like a star, hitting two sixes – balls that fell outside the boundary – and three fours, along with some single runs. However, having given a dazzling performance and accrued thirty-three runs, Charles began to feel invincible. In the next second, it was over. He swung the bat too hard, clipped the ball and was caught out by the wicket keeper.

As the next man went in to bat, Charles walked off the pitch, took off his pads and sat down in a wicker chair at the edge of the field, slightly apart from everyone else. He gazed out at the match, angry that he had been caught out by an error of judgement.

What a stupid stroke, he thought. I should never have swung at that ball like that. It was wide – and I should have left it . . .

He was still simmering when Ariel came up and plopped down beside him on the grass.

'Hi,' she said, looking up at him with her big grey eyes.

'Hi,' he replied and continued to stare out at the match.

Ariel hugged her legs and watched the cricketers. Then, completely out of the blue, she said, 'You don't have to be a "bad" Sprite, Charles.'

'Oh!' he said. He blinked and looked down at her, astonished by her lack of guile.

Ariel was silent. Then she asked, 'What did you see in the

portal? Did you see the arch behind George?'

Charles smiled. 'Yes, I did,' he replied, as Ariel looked up at him.

'And did you smell the roses?'

'Yes,' he said. 'I smelled the roses.'

They sat silent again.

Then Ariel asked, 'What does the portal mean?'

Charles screwed up his face and said, 'Mean? I'm not sure what it means. I think it could be a way to go back into Sprite family time.'

'George led us in . . .' said Ariel.

'Yes, it did feel like that,' agreed Charles. 'And out!'

Ariel laughed, then said, 'What's the point of the portal? It's jolly interesting and all that, but what will it *do*?'

'Well, if you could go back in time, maybe it would allow people to right some wrongs,' suggested Charles. 'Put things right. That sort of stuff.'

'I'd probably make things worse!' Ariel grinned.

Charles laughed. 'Yes, you might do!'

'Do you think we could put Glenda right?' asked Ariel, catching his gaze.

'Hmm, tough call,' said Charles. 'If you could do *that*, you could probably change the world. She's a pretty nasty woman.'

'Yes, we know,' said Ariel. 'She keeps trying to hurt us.'

Charles looked down at the grass. 'Yes – I'm sorry,' he said.

'Flame says you're a pawn in Glenda's game,' said Ariel.

'Does she?' Charles bit his bottom lip. 'Hmm.'

'She says you should be a knight, not a pawn,' said Ariel. 'Pawns can only move forward, she says, but knights can move all ways. But I don't know – I don't play chess.'

Charles smiled. 'Knights are brave,' he said.

'Aren't you?'

'No, I'm rather weak,' he grimaced.

'I don't think people know if they're brave or not till they have to be,' said Ariel.

'How do you mean?'

'It's not the sort of thing you know till you've had to be it. Brave, I mean.'

'Are you brave?' he asked.

She nodded. 'I have been. I was brave when Glenda attacked us at the concert – and then again at the house the other week, when she tried to bring the roof down. We were all very brave.'

'What happened?' asked Charles, sitting forward.

'She attacked the house while Mum and Dad were away,' said Ariel. 'The roof nearly fell in and the towers nearly collapsed. Grandma was hurt and Ash's rabbit was killed. It was very, very scary.'

'Good Lord,' said Charles quietly. 'I didn't know that.'

'But the point is, I didn't know I was brave until Glenda came along,' continued Ariel. 'I'd never had to be brave before. It's like you – you probably haven't been a good person before, but it doesn't mean to say you can't be.'

Charles smiled. 'No,' he agreed. 'It doesn't.'

'So are you going to try to be a "good" person?' asked Ariel.

'I'll let you know,' he said, thoughtfully. 'You'll have to let me think about that one.'

'Okay then,' she said and got up. 'I'm going to get some elderflower cordial. Would you like some?'

'Yes, please,' said Charles.

When she returned with the cordial, Ariel said, 'When did you get your magic power?'

Charles gasped in surprise and looked around. Would anybody hear? It seemed not – nobody turned around.

'Shh, Ariel,' he said.

'Sorry,' she whispered, sitting down on the grass. 'Well?'

'When I was twelve,' he said, quietly. 'And you?'

'On my ninth birthday – like my sisters,' said Ariel. 'The same time as Glenda Glass moved to The Oaks. It was as if she moved here especially.'

'She did,' said Charles.

Ariel sat up and stared at him. 'How did she know?'

Charles shook his head. 'I don't know. I wish I knew how she knew things about us all.'

'Are you going to tell her all about us?' Ariel asked.

Charles breathed in deeply. 'I already have,' he said softly.

'Oh!' said Ariel, her eyes full of hurt. 'That wasn't very kind of you.'

'No,' he said.

'At least you have been honest.' For a few seconds, Ariel watched the match in silence, then turned back to Charles. 'Did you tell Glenda about Ash's magic stone? It's funny you heard it squeaking and we didn't.'

Charles bit his lip and nodded.

Suddenly, there was a lot of clapping. Harry the farmer walked on to the crease.

'What's happening?' asked Ariel.

'Harry's going in to bat – and he's our eighth man,' replied Charles. 'Things are looking bleak for us.'

'Why?' asked Ariel.

'Because we've only scored 115 runs and have only three men left – and they're likely to be our weaker batsmen,' explained Charles, rubbing his chin.

'How many runs have we got to beat?' asked Ariel.

'159,' replied Charles. 'That's another thirty-five. I don't think we'll do it.'

'Harry will sort them out,' said Ariel. 'He's Dad's "secret weapon".'

And he was. Solid and unflappable, Harry hit the ball back for the next three-quarters of an hour in a manner almost tediously reliable. But it did the trick. The Aussies just could not get rid of him and, one by one, he racked up the runs. The match concluded when he hit his first four, giving the English team a score of 162 runs.

Charles and Ariel jumped up. 'Yeah!' they cried.

Everybody clapped. 'Good play!' they shouted and, 'Well done!' as the teams walked off the field.

Dad was over the moon.

'You did it, Dad!' said Flame, giving him a hug.

'I didn't think we would!' he laughed. 'It was so close!'

He and Geoff shook hands and bashed each other on the back.

'Good on yer,' said Geoff, laughing. 'We'll get you next year, you wait and see!'

Cans of cold drink were opened and sweaty brows rubbed with towels. The cricketers relaxed and the party started.

Flame found Quinn and stood, waiting, as one of the other fathers wished him well. Then he turned to her and grinned.

Her cheeks flushed and she gave him the widest smile. 'Well done,' she said. 'You were amazing!'

'Thank you,' he said, watching her green eyes. 'So were you!'

Flame drew breath. *He's looking at me*, she thought. He's looking at me!

Just then Ariel came up. 'Mum wants you,' she said to Flame. Then she smiled up at Quinn. 'Hi,' she said.

'Hi, Ariel,' said Quinn. 'You look very pretty.'

'Thank you,' she twinkled.

Urgh, thought Flame. It always happens. Just as I get Quinn to myself . . .

'Better go and help Mum,' she said to Quinn.

'Sure – catch you later,' he said.

Sprite Towers was alive with life and enjoyment. The barbecue sizzled. Glasses chinked. People laughed and the conversation flowed.

Dad put his arm around Mum and gave her a contented kiss on the cheek. Anne and Geoff laughed with their friends. Jamie chatted up Flame's friend, Pia. Lottie giggled with Vivek. Ash, Ariel and Daniel kneeled in the Secret Garden, watching a huge toad that had crawled out from behind a stone.

On the side of the terrace, Grandma stood and watched her family and their friends with a deep sense of pride and happiness. Seeing her there, Flame turned and walked towards her.

'You look nice, love,' said Grandma, admiring the skirt and pretty top Flame was now wearing.

'Thank you,' smiled Flame. 'Has Charles left?'

'Yes, a little while ago.'

'I wonder where all this leaves us with Glenda,' said Flame.

'We'll just have to wait and see,' said Grandma. 'You all did well this week and I'm proud of you.'

'Thank you, Grandma,' said Flame, and she gave her a big hug.

And, as the Sprite family partied on, Charles Smythson drove towards London. When the road wound through the forest, he turned off the radio and stared into the inky dark, his mind racing and whirring. He thought of the Sprites – his own family, no less – and of all the things that had happened in the last twelve days.

In the boot of the car were two photographic umbrellas, two sets of lights and a suitcase. On the back seat lay a smart leather bag, in which were a camera containing dozens of photographs, several pens and a black notebook.

On the front seat beside him were a plate of food and two

cans of drink, which Ottalie Sprite, ever thoughtful, had insisted he take for the journey in case he got hungry or thirsty.

As mile after mile of trees passed by in the night, Charles's mind began to calm. As it did so, he realised that in his heart he felt growing a little seed of doubt.

At Sprite Towers, the night air was fragrant with the smell of lavender and roses. For a few minutes, the Sprite Sisters withdrew from the party and came together on the wide rolling lawn. Spontaneously – as if with one mind – they grabbed each others' hands and began to run sideways in a circle, getting faster and faster and faster, until at last they were going so quickly that they all fell over in a heap, laughing. Then they lay back on the grass to catch their breath and watched the clouds swoosh across the moon, a thin crescent of silver rising in the August sky.

SPECIAL THANKS

Big thanks to all the Piccadilly Press team for their skill, effort and enthusiasm especially Brenda Gardner, Melissa Hyder, Mary Byrne, Margot Edwards, Vivien Tesseras and Victoria Lee, the copy editor. Particular thanks to my whizz' editor, Anne Clark, for her sharp eyes and sound judgment. Also to Chris Winn for bringing the Sprite world to life in his drawing and to Anna Gould and Simon Davis for their third striking cover.

Big thanks, too, to my agent, Veronique Baxter at David Higham Associates, and her assistant, Laura West.

Thank you to Sarah Skinner at Norwich Waterstone's for her continued and wonderful support of the Sprite Sisters, and to Elaine Simpson at Norwich Millennium Library.

Charlotte Crawley's advice on country house art inventories and Henry Crawley's advice on gardening has been invaluable. Thank you, Crawleys! So too, has been Alex Winn's advice on farming.

A big thank you to my parents and friends for their support and to Rosie, Alex & Hils for their boundless enthusiasm.

Lastly, Sprite Sister fans – great big thanks to you all, especially Rose Medler, Alice Stuttaford and Amelia Johnson.

Keep Spriting!